JFICTION
Macke
Mackel, Kathy.

MadCat /

MADCAT

Kathy Mackel

🔳 HARPERCOLLINS*PUBLISHERS*

MadCat

Copyright © 2005 by Kathy Mackel

Library of Congress Cataloging-in-Publication Data
Mackel, Kathy.
   MadCat / Kathy Mackel.—1st ed.
      p.   cm.
   Summary: Fastpitch softball catcher MadCat Campione's love for the
sport—and her relationship with her best friends—is strained when her team
competes on a national level.
   ISBN 0-06-054869-X — ISBN 0-06-054870-3 (lib. bdg.)
   [1. Softball—Fiction.   2. Friendship—Fiction.]   I. Title.
PZ7.M1955Ma 2005   2004006618
[Fic]—dc22

Typography by Sasha Illingworth
3 4 5 6 7 8 9 10
❖
First Edition

To Leah, who always plays the game
the way it should be played

To the memory of Mike Coppinger,
who made sure the game was always fair
and always for the kids

STING
SOFTBALL
TRYOUTS

Norwich Sting Girls Softball announces tryouts for its 12-and-under tournament team. Any girl age 12 or younger as of January 1st of this year is eligible to try out.

The Sting play competitive fastpitch softball from May through Labor Day in weekend tournaments throughout New England. For information, call Ginny Page, President of the Board of Directors . . .

Chapter ONE

I was so mad, I could spit.

But if I asked for a time-out, Coach MacMahon and my mother would kill me.

"Madelyn Catherine!" Mom would gasp. "Ladies don't spit in public."

"Focus, MadCat," Mac would growl.

Mugger flapped her mitt at me from behind home plate. Mugger's real name was Amanda Murphy. She had carrot-red hair and a ton of freckles.

"It makes her sound like a criminal," my mother said when I announced that I had changed Amanda's name to Mugger.

"Good," I said. "You gotta be tough to play fastpitch softball."

Mugger's grin was frozen under the catcher's mask. This was her first time catching. But this was my first time pitching, so we were even, except that she was scared and I was mad.

I drove my arms upward, stepped long, and windmilled. *CLANG!* The ball slammed high up the backstop!

"Ball four!" the umpire yelled.

Batter on first, no outs. It was the seventh inning and my team, the Norwich Sting, was ahead, four to zero. This scrimmage against the Granite State Bombers was a chance for girls trying out for both teams to show their stuff. We had ten girls returning from last year, which left two open positions. Because the game didn't count for anything beyond tryouts, Coach felt comfortable yanking our starter, Jessica Page, and putting me in to pitch in the last inning.

Jess Page had been my best friend forever, and the Sting's number one pitcher for three years. No one was going to bump her from the roster. But when Hannah Stamos moved to Utah last October, the number two pitching spot opened up. I had been working my butt off all winter to fill that opening.

"Why are you messing around with pitching?" Mac had asked. "You're the best catcher in your age group in New Hampshire."

Twelve years old and I was already stereotyped.

"Because," I said.

Because I was sick of squatting in the dust. Sweating under twenty pounds of equipment. Eating all the bad balls. Watching the pitcher get all the glory.

Because it was time for MadCat Campione to step out of the catcher's box and into the sunshine.

The batter leaned over the plate and smirked at me. I whipped my best fastball inside. Too far inside. The batter dropped her bat and grabbed her butt.

"Sorry," I mumbled. Two batters on, no outs. And I hadn't pitched a strike yet.

"You can do it, Lily," my mother sang from the first base line.

You can do it, MadCat, Mellissa's voice echoed in my head. Mellissa Kubit was pitching for the high school on this Saturday morning. But her teaching stayed with me. *Relax. Breathe. Let the explosion build from the inside. Pivot, push, leap, snap—*

"Stee-r-r-r-ike!" the umpire yelled.

Yes! My first strike in a real game! I hoped Mom had caught it on tape so Bump could see it. My father watched all my games on videotape these days.

I wound up, threw and—*BAM!* The ball whacked the umpire in the face mask, and careened down the third base line.

"She's going!" someone yelled.

I dove into the fence in front of the third base dugout and dug the ball out of the dirt.

"Home!" someone yelled.

I whipped the ball. A perfect throw, right to Mugger.

The ball rolled out of Mugger's glove as she went down for the tag.

"Safe!" the ump yelled.

Mugger walked the ball out to me. "Sorry," she stammered. Her face was shiny red, like a radish.

I wanted to strangle her. Instead, I said, "Never mind. You're doing great."

The sun was high in the sky and the air was sweet and warm, an amazing April day for New Hampshire. The fences were packed with people. The game might be meaningless but making a fastpitch tournament team meant everything.

I focused, and struck out the next batter. Then I walked two to load the bases.

"Working hard, MadCat," Ginny Page called from over her scorebook. Ginny was Jess's mom and the President of the Sting.

Working hard is what adults say when you're stinking up the ballpark.

I stepped and pitched. The ball floated to the plate like I was serving it on Mom's china platter. *WHAM!* The batter banged it right at my head!

SMACK! It hit my glove like a missile but I held it tight.

Jess Page was at the foul line, calling, "Time-out!" The umpire took off her face mask, frowned at Jess, then waved her to the pitcher's circle.

"This is all your fault!" I said. Jess was the one who had talked me into taking up pitching.

She laughed. "I told you it's harder than it looks. But you're doing great."

"Oh yeah. I'm great at stinking."

"Come on, MadCat. What do you always tell me when I'm in a pickle?"

"Deep breath. Cool head. Focus on one pitch at a time," I recited.

"You got it. So just do it." Jess patted my shoulder, then walked out of the circle. She froze halfway to the dugout.

Bridget Ryan was stepping up to the plate. Jess looked at her, then back at me, her eyes wide. "*Duck*," Jess mouthed, then ran into the dugout, laughing.

Bridget Ryan was shaped like a turtle and moved about as fast. But if Bridget Ryan blasted the ball at my head, you'd see daylight between my ears.

Forget the cool head. I just wanted to keep the one I had on my shoulders.

I pitched. *CRACK!* The ball shot to center field. *CLANG!* It whacked the fence, then ricocheted past Casey in the outfield. The bases were clearing—one, two, then three runners in. Score tied and Nina was still running down the ball in deep right. Meanwhile, Bridget chugged her way from second to third.

"Cut!" I yelled. Nina whipped a long strike to me. I whipped the ball to home plate. A perfect throw, but Mugger was positioned too far back. The ball chipped the front of home plate and bounced up.

Mugger reached for it—with her throwing hand.

"No!" I yelled.

SLAP! Mugger shrieked with pain. The ball rolled into

the infield. Bridget Ryan slid into home plate, huffing like a hurricane.

Game over.

Final score: Five to four, Bombers over the Sting.

Important stats: I stunk as pitcher. I lost us the game. I broke Mugger's finger.

I was so disgusted, I decided to spit.

Chapter TWO

Mothers can say a thousand words without opening their mouths.

As we tromped into the kitchen, Mom flicked her left eyebrow. My father nodded and the discussion about my game was left for later. "Hey, Cat," Bump said, smiling. "How about doing some digging?"

"I suppose," I mumbled.

Bump is my name for my father. What was supposed to be *Poppa* when I was a baby, turned out to be *Bumpa*, which got shortened to *Bump*.

My real name is Madelyn Catherine Campione. Mom tries to call me Madelyn but I object so she settles for whatever flower comes into her mind. I don't know which is worse—Madelyn or Begonia.

Bump calls me Cat. A compromise, he says, to keep family peace.

I named myself MadCat when Jess and I joined the Sting. I was the youngest player on the team—only eight—and I wanted something to make me sound real tough.

"It makes you sound deranged," my mother said, the first time she heard it.

"Good," I said, even though I wasn't sure what deranged meant.

Madelyn was someone who did her nails and never had a bad hair day. Madelyn was someone who everyone's parents liked to have over for dinner so they could yak about her perfect manners to their rotten kids. Madelyn was someone you opened a door for.

MadCat was someone you got out of the way for. And that goes a long, long way in fastpitch softball.

I slumped upstairs to change.

"Wear long pants!" Bump yelled after me.

While I was gone, Mom would fill Bump in on how much I stunk at pitching. Then we could go bury the dust of a very bad game in our very good garden.

● ● ● ● ●

Ten minutes later, I met Bump out at the shed. "How come you told me to wear jeans?" I asked. "It's broiling out here."

Bump swung open the door. "Because you're going to run the Nag this year."

The Nag—our eight-horsepower rototiller—was so powerful it chewed through weeds, rocks, and soil like I plow through chocolate frosting on birthday cake. Every spring, I begged to run the monster. And every spring Bump said, "Too big, too powerful, too dangerous."

But not today. I pushed the snowblower and sand buckets aside so I could drag the Nag out of its winter resting spot. When the Nag was all gassed up, I rolled her out to what Mom called our "lower forty."

Our house has a small front lawn, bordered by a stone wall and perennial flowers that bloom from snowmelt to snowfall. In March we have purple crocuses; in April, yellow daffodils; in May, white lilies. In June, the bigheaded peonies reign over the green shoots of the daylilies.

Summer is a jumble of flowers, buzzing bees, and singing birds. In September, tall sunflowers wave yellow while plump marigolds burst with gold. Then we fade through the fall with the dignified pinks and lavenders of hardy mums.

Mom is in charge of the flowers. "Feeding our souls," she calls it.

The lower forty is beyond the brick patio in our backyard—Bump's sun-filled plot of vegetables. Beyond the garden is a patch of apple, cherry, and pear trees.

While Mom feeds our souls, Bump and I feed our bellies. It begins every April, when we turn over the soil to get ready to plant.

I pushed open the choke and turned the starter. The

Nag bucked forward, then slowed to a crawl.

The rows mounted up quickly. Back and forth, the Nag plowed up the sleeping soil. My thoughts rolled like the dirt. *So what if I'm not a great pitcher?* Kids would kill to make the Sting. And kids who did make the team would kill to get off the bench and play all the time, like I got to.

I would apologize to Mellissa for wasting her time with this pitching nonsense, and just get on with being the best twelve-year-old catcher in New Hampshire.

With that seed planted, I let my thoughts tumble into the coming summer. If it didn't rain soon, every infield in New England would be a dust bowl. Every time someone laid down a bunt, it would spin in the dust like a tornado. Every time a batter dug in at the plate, I'd get a face full of clay.

Another summer eating dirt.

PUM! A tiny stone bounced off my backside. I looked around. Bump waved his arms back and forth. I flipped off the Nag. She sputtered, then went quiet.

"I only did half the garden," I said. "There's plenty of time to finish the rest before supper."

"You don't need to. This is all we're doing this year."

"But why . . . ?" I said. Suddenly all the thoughts tumbling in my head screeched to a halt. I'd been so busy worrying about myself, I buried something else deep—something far worse than me stinking as a pitcher. Something I realized I'd been ignoring all day. Maybe all week.

I hosed off the Nag, then pushed her back to the shed. I stuck my face under the water, washing off dust and sweat.

When I had stunk at pitching this morning, my gut had been ripped out. Now my heart was being ripped out, now that I knew why I got to run the Nag. Why we were only putting in half a garden this year.

Bump hadn't gotten out of his wheelchair once today.

Which meant he might never get out of that wheelchair again. I didn't think I could dig that thought deep enough to ever make it grow into something good.

Chapter THREE

Mellissa Kubit was everything I would give my left toes to be. Tall. Blond. Slender. Pretty. An incredible pitcher.

I was everything Mellissa would probably give her right toes not to be. Round-faced and stumpy-legged. Mousy-haired and big-eyed. Condemned to be a dust-eating catcher for the rest of my life.

Mellissa had stopped by to watch the videotape of my pitching performance. After I finished rototilling, we went for a jog.

"Want to tell me about today?" she asked. She wasn't breathing hard, even though we were halfway to the center of Norwich.

"What's there to tell? You saw the tape—I stunk."

"Did you hear those words come out of my mouth?" Mellissa said.

"You're thinking it."

"What I'm thinking is that you didn't do too bad for your first time," she said.

"Not bad? I gave up five runs in one inning! Never even got the third out!"

"The first game I ever pitched, I only gave up two runs," Mellissa said.

"See! I told you I stink!" I yelped.

Mellissa laughed. "That's because my coach yanked me before someone arrested me for assault. I hit five batters in a row!" She was breathing a little harder now. "You have to stick with it, MadCat. Pitching takes time and patience."

"Yeah, well, patience is for old people," I said. My lungs felt like they were about to burst. We turned into the park. A winter chill swept in on a sudden gust from the northwest. Snow was in the air, even though pockets of sunlight still held the day's warmth.

In New Hampshire, the weather could change in an instant.

"So how did you do today?" I asked.

"I pitched a no-hitter." Mellissa's voice was as calm as if she had just said "I use mint toothpaste."

I skidded to stop. "That's awesome!"

Mellissa jogged a circle around me. "No, it's not. We lost."

"How could you pitch a no-hitter and lose?"

"Come on, MadCat. Think." Mellissa headed off across the soccer field.

I ran after her. "A walk? Followed by a mess on the bases?"

"You got it," Mellissa said. "Runner steals second. Next pitch, she goes for third. My catcher whips it into left field. Runner scores. We don't. We lose, one to zip."

"Bummer," I said.

"Things don't always work out the way you want them to," Mellissa said. "Right?"

Mellissa sprinted for the playground. I panted, trying to keep up. The sweat on my face turned icy cold. The sun was almost down.

"Do you think I'm not going to show up for my next game just because we blew this one?" she said when I finally caught up to her.

"No. That would be stupid," I panted.

"Why?"

"Because you worked too hard to give up," I said, too fast.

She grabbed the back of my shirt. "So have you," she said.

I pulled away. "A lot of good it did me."

"Stop being a baby. You had a rough outing, that's all. That's the game."

Mellissa dropped onto a swing and pushed off. She was airborne in two strides. I took the swing next to her; it took me five pushes to swing high. We swung until the stars came out.

Then we ran hard back to my house, trying to warm up again. Mellissa climbed into her pickup truck. "Well, MadCat. Guess I'll see you around," she said.

"Right," I said.

"Right about seeing you around?"

"Right about everything," I said.

Mellissa laughed, then drove away.

I could smell the fresh soil from the garden. The temperature had dropped twenty-five degrees since this morning's game, but it didn't matter.

Summer was in the air.

Chapter FOUR

Some ignorant folks might say Mugger Murphy lived in a junkyard. But some ignorant folks don't know the difference between a bulldozer and a backhoe, so who were they to judge?

Mugger was the luckiest kid in the world, to live among this wonderland of mowers, blowers, tractors, fenders, and truck axles. I would never get bored living in a place like that.

The Murphys' house—a double-wide blue trailer with silver trim—was hidden behind a row of scrub pines. A screened-in porch covered the front door. The window boxes were filled with faded silk flowers.

I'll have to bring over some of our bulbs, I thought as I dropped my bike in the driveway. *Show Mugger how to grow real flowers.*

It was Sunday afternoon. Mom was working at the hospital, and Bump was messing around in the shed. I had ridden my bike across town to ask Mugger a favor.

Mugger came to the door, licking a Popsicle. Her mouth was ringed in pale pink; she looked like a little kid who tried to put on lipstick but missed by a half mile all around.

"Hey," I said. "What's happening?"

"Hey," Mugger smiled, then shrugged. "Nothing."

Her Popsicle dripped down her hand. "Want one?" she asked, wiping the pink drops onto her white T-shirt.

"Sure," I said.

"We only had grape left," she said a minute later. "Hope that's okay." She sat down on the front steps.

"That's cool. I like grape." I sat down with her. "How's the finger?" Mugger's ring finger was taped into a splint; the tape was pink with Popsicle juice.

Mugger shrugged. "Okay."

"Sorry I broke it," I said.

"Turns out it's just jammed."

"Cool," I said.

"Cool," Mugger echoed. "Still hurts, though."

I swallowed the last chunk of my Popsicle whole, ignoring the sharp freeze in my belly. "So, I came over to ask if you'd want to catch for me," I said.

"Right now?" Mugger's eyes went wide, then squished together as she smiled. The kid would smile if her hair were on fire.

"Maybe in a couple of days," I said. "When your finger is better."

"So you mean . . . like fooling-around catch? Or warm-up catch?"

"Catch-catch. You know, shinpads, helmet and mask, chest protector. While I practice pitching, you can practice catching. Wouldn't that be cool?"

Mugger smiled and shrugged. "I don't want to break any more fingers."

"You said it wasn't broken!"

"It could have been."

"That's because you don't know how to catch right," I said. "I'll teach you how. Okay? Hey, why don't we practice every Tuesday and Thursday? That way it won't interfere with our Sting practices."

Mugger sucked all the juice off her Popsicle sticks, then stuck them in her back pocket. "How come you're asking me? Why don't you ask someone else?"

I had asked someone else. Jess was too busy with basketball, pitching lessons, and golf. Nina refused flat out. Tori played the piano and had that can't-risk-my-fingers thing. Jenna was afraid Coach Mac would get mad.

"You're my first choice, 'cuz you'd make a great catcher," I said.

"Okay," she shrugged. "I guess I don't have anything better to do."

Chapter FIVE

The smoke alarm screamed. I froze in the breezeway, debating whether to run to the neighbors and call the Fire Department or to go into the house and strangle the darn thing.

Smoke filled the kitchen. But the curtains, paper towels, napkins, and other flammables weren't burning. Then I spotted the flames—inside the oven.

My supper was baking to more than a crisp.

I went inside and jumped high to yank the smoke alarm out of the ceiling. The detectors in the basement and upstairs were silent. Okay, that confirmed the rest of the house wasn't on fire. Just the roast chicken Mom had left us.

I cranked open the window over the sink. The smoke shooshed out. Fresh, icy air rushed in. Outside, a cold rain fell.

"Bump?" I yelled. "Where are you? We got a problem here!"

I doubled up the pot holders, then carefully pulled the smoking mess out of the oven. What was supposed to be an herb-marinated chicken was now a mass of black. Where was my father? He'd been so tired all week—maybe he had slept through the smoke alarm.

My feet barely touched the steps as I flew up the stairs. "Bump? Where the heck are you?"

I flung open the door to my parents' bedroom. Empty.

The rain drummed on the roof. Turning now to sleet, I realized by the hard *tat-tat-tat*. Typical New Hampshire— one day you're frying, the next day you're freezing. I was glad I had made it back from Mugger's before this crummy weather hit.

I slid open the door to my parents' upstairs deck. Ice pelted my face as I peered out at the backyard. A dark lump sat in the middle of the garden.

"Bump!" I screamed.

My father lifted his left arm in a lazy wave. Why was he sitting there? Why didn't he come in?

Because he can't, I realized.

•   •   •   •   •

Bump's wheelchair was stuck in the wet soil. He was shaking so hard, I thought the darn thing would collapse.

"I didn't realize how loose the soil was." Bump's teeth

clicked-clicked from the cold. "The wheels got stuck."

I put my arms around his waist and yanked. "Come on, let's get you inside." In sweatpants and windbreaker, my father shivered so hard I thought he'd rattle his bones through his skin.

We inched out of the garden, toward the house. "How long were you stuck out there?" I asked.

"Since three-thirty," Bump mumbled. "I wanted to get the snow peas in."

"Why didn't you shout for help? The Monroes are home."

Bump tightened his grip on me. "You know why."

That blasted Campione pride. He had it. I had it. Mom hated it. "It makes rational people do ridiculous things," she always said.

Bump stayed in the shower for what seemed like forever. Then he came out, he wrapped himself in an old robe and sat in his recliner.

Meanwhile, I tried to salvage supper. I thawed a jar of plum tomatoes in the microwave and peeled the black skin off the chicken carcass. Deep in the breast were about four ounces of unburned meat. I diced the chicken, simmered it in the tomatoes with some of our dried basil and oregano, then served it over angel-hair pasta.

I brought Bump's plate into the family room. Even though the television was on, he was staring out the window. The sleet had streaked the glass with ice.

"I made you supper," I said.

"I'm not hungry."

"You've got to eat," I said.

"Not now," he said, pulling the blanket up to his face. "I'm too tired."

"I can help you," I said.

CLUNK! The recliner flipped upright. "I said no!" Bump snapped. Then he collapsed back into the chair, pulling the blanket over him.

I took the plate back out to the kitchen, sprinkled some hot pepper and Parmesan cheese over the sauce, then dug my fork in.

But I didn't feel much like eating either.

Chapter SIX

You're not supposed to damn people to hell. I don't know if the same rule applies to diseases but I didn't care—as I dug Bump's wheelchair out of the garden, I damned his stupid multiple sclerosis straight to hell.

I was four years old when Bump was diagnosed with multiple sclerosis. Back then, Bump was Lieutenant Phil Campione of the Manchester Police Department. On a hot August day, he and his officers served warrants on a suspected drug operation. The bad guys burst out of that old house like rats running for the gutter.

Bump's running through backyards, jumping fences, dodging dogs, his eyes on the perp. Suddenly everything goes black, like someone dropped a bag over his head.

His fellow officers found him a minute later, stumbling

around and rubbing his eyes. His vision came back after about a half an hour. They thought it might be heatstroke or an allergic reaction to something in the drug house. Whatever it was, it was over and everyone had a nervous laugh about Phil Campione playing "pin the tail on the bad guy" without a blindfold.

A few weeks later, my father dropped a hot cup of coffee in the lap of the Chief of Police. Bump was assigned to desk duty and made the rounds of the doctors until they agreed on multiple sclerosis.

The official nickname for the disease is MS. I have my own term for it, but it's a swear word so I'm not allowed to say it. But anytime Bump is having a bad time, I think it. Like now, as I dragged his chair to the shed so I could wash the mud out of the wheels.

Most people with MS get to keep their jobs. Bump didn't.

Most people with MS don't end up in wheelchairs. It looked like Bump was going to.

Most people with MS lead normal lives. Bump always said he didn't care about a normal life—not when he had such a wonderful life with Mom and me.

But now I had to wonder as I dug Bump's chair out of the garden—was that wonderful life about to be buried too deep for us to make it ever bloom again?

● ● ● ● ●

When I walked into the family room, Mom lounged on the sofa, still in her hospital scrubs. Bump hadn't gotten out of the recliner.

"So, how was the chicken?" Mom asked.

"Um . . ." I glanced at Bump. He squeezed his eyes shut. "I forgot about it, and it kinda burnt to a crisp."

"Madelyn Catherine! I stuffed it with wild rice and shiitake mushrooms. You know how expensive they are."

"I'm sorry. Really. I went off on my bike and just forgot. Jerk, huh?"

"Not a jerk." Mom sighed. "Just a kid."

"Your mom and I were just having a discussion," Bump said.

My breath caught in my throat. *Here it comes,* I thought. *We're going to talk about the wheelchair.* "About what?"

"Ginny Page called while you were outside," he said. "You made the team, of course."

Mom took over. "The Board of Directors wants to take the Sting to a higher level of play this summer."

"Huh? We were third in the state last year!" I said.

"They want you to go National this year," Mom said.

Go National? That meant being the best in the state, the best in New England. That meant traveling to a big softball state like California or Texas to play the best teams in the country. Going National was as awesome as fastpitch softball could get.

"Cool!" I said.

"You need to think carefully before you agree to

participate," my mother said. "It will mean more practices, more tournaments. Then, if the team wins a berth, it means a trip to Kentucky for the National Fastpitch Softball World Series."

In a flash I was in my Sting uniform, squatting behind the plate. Jess whipped in fastballs. The California girls squealed, the Texas girls sweated, the Arizona girls cursed. The Sting of little Norwich, New Hampshire, stomped them all.

"We told Ginny it was your decision," Bump said.

"No-brainer, then. I'll do it!"

"It will be practices every night, Daisy," Mom said. "Tournaments every weekend. No more going to the beach or pool parties or sleepovers. Do you really want to devote your whole spring and summer to softball?"

"Are you kidding?" I jumped out of my chair and grabbed the phone.

"Where are you going, Cat?" Bump called.

"I gotta call Jess!" I was speed-dialing as I left the room.

It wasn't until late that night, after I had fantasized with Jess and Erin and Tori about winning a National trophy that I realized I hadn't called Mugger.

Chapter SEVEN

I woke up to a world wrapped in ice. It was the third week in April, the first day of spring vacation. Two days ago I sweated my butt off in the scrimmage and now I could cruise the neighborhood in my ice skates.

Good old New Hampshire.

Mom and Bump were still asleep. I steamed whole-grain grits, and blended in Bump's pear preserves, topped with brown sugar. I poured three glasses of our home-pressed apple juice, then headed upstairs with a tray.

"Come in," Bump called. I pushed in and set the tray on the bed between them.

Mom was just hanging up the phone. "You have practice today."

"Wrong number," I laughed. "I don't play ice hockey.

Or was that my bobsled coach who called?"

"Softball, Tulip."

"Good one, Mom. But April Fool's was two weeks ago."

"Madelyn Catherine. Ginny Page called a practice for this afternoon, after the roads get sanded."

"What the heck? We're gonna play in the ice?"

It was Mom's turn to laugh. "Not exactly."

• • • • •

No kidding *not exactly*. After lunch, Mom drove me up to Manchester. When we walked into the field house of Middlesex College, I knew I was in heaven.

Stretched out before me, like my wildest dream, was an indoor softball diamond. The infield was light clay and perfectly groomed—not a rock or ditch anywhere. The turf outfield was greener than my front lawn in June.

I gasped. "This is so awesome."

"Maybe a bit too awesome," Mom snapped.

"What? Why do you say that?"

"Nothing." Mom gave me a hug and a quick kiss. "I hope you have fun, Begonia."

She *hoped* I would have fun? I would *absolutely* have fun, playing softball inside while the world outside was covered in ice.

Jess came running over to meet me. "Ever seen a place like this?"

I pretended to be unimpressed. "What a dump!"

She punched me. "How can you say that?"

I bit my lip, trying not to laugh. "Easy. Where's the concession stand? How can I play softball without my sausage sub and that fungus they pass off as peppers?"

Jess nodded slowly. "I know what you mean, Madelyn. It's an absolute disgrace, making us play in conditions like this. I mean, how can I survive without my onion rings fried in last week's grease?"

"And consider this, Jessica. No pancake-flat cheeseburgers that are still frozen in the middle!"

"No hard-rock doughnuts left over from the day before yesterday!"

"And while we're talking about old and used food—no smelly Porta Potties! How absolutely appalling," I said, putting my nose in the air.

"You mean that we have to use flush toilets? How absolutely pathetic!" Jess said, her hands to her cheeks and her mouth in an *O*.

"I'm not even sure I'll remember how to flush."

"I simply do not know how they expect us to play in conditions like these."

"How absolutely primitive," I said in my most stuck-up voice.

Jess doubled over in laughter. She got me started, and we howled together, tears running down our cheeks.

I had never been so absolutely happy in my life, I decided.

• • • • •

I had never been so miserable in my life.

Coach Mac had the six of us doing laps around the field. "This stinks!" I squealed. My ribs felt like there were tomato stakes sticking through them.

"Stop whining." Jess wasn't even panting. She was a basketball star, too, and was used to pounding her legs through the floor.

"I shouldn't have eaten that five-alarm chili for lunch," Jenna moaned. "I'm gonna puke!"

"I'm gonna chase Mac around the parking lot until he pukes," Nikki swore. We all laughed. Nikki weighed about seventy pounds sweating wet. Before he retired, Coach Mac had been a prison guard.

"So what's the deal with all these laps?" Erin said, fanning her T-shirt to dry her underarms.

"Ugh! Haven't you ever heard of deodorant?" Tori howled. "Your pits smell worse than Jenna's chili breath!"

"All part of the plan to get the Sting to Nationals," Jess said.

"What, Jenna's pukey breath?" I asked. "Or Erin's pits?"

"It's called *conditioning*," Jess sneered. "You might want to try it sometime, instead of vegging out in front of your video games."

"Hey!" Tori glared. "My thumbs can take your thumbs anytime!" We all laughed, except Jenna, who was too busy burping.

"Casey and those guys are late," Jenna huffed. "Mac better make them do twice as many laps as we have to do."

"Casey and those guys aren't late," Jess said. "They aren't coming."

I skidded to a stop. "Why not?"

Jess kept running. "You'll see!"

Coach Mac waved us to a stop. He had joined the Sting twenty years ago, when his daughters played fastpitch softball. They grew up and left the game but Mac stayed.

"Where's everyone else?" Nikki snapped.

Mac motioned across the infield, to the first base side. "Here they are now."

I did such a sharp double-take, I almost sprained my head.

Bridget Ryan was the first one in, carrying her bat bag and wearing her blue Bombers' jacket. She was followed by four more girls. I didn't know their names but I knew their faces and where they liked their pitches—we had played against these girls for years.

"What are those kids doing here?" I said.

"They're your teammates," Mac said.

"What!" I squealed. "Where's Ashley? Mugger? And the others?"

Mac rubbed his face, looking pained. "The Board was supposed to explain to you girls." He looked at Jess like it was her fault.

She just shrugged. "I guess Mom thought you would tell everyone, Coach."

"Tell us what?" Nikki demanded.

"Some of your . . . former . . . teammates are pursuing other options this year," Mac said.

Other options was a polite way of saying Sting players had been cut to make room for these zucchinis. Cutting almost half of my team was like cutting out the ground under my feet. And who did these new girls think they were, coming from out of town to play for Norwich?

What kind of team would this be, now that the Sting was going National?

Chapter EIGHT

Coach Mac waved the two groups together in the middle of the infield.

"You all know Bridget Ryan," he said. "Best hitter I've ever seen." Bridget blushed and looked at her feet.

Mac nodded at two girls. "Leigha and Kayleigh Loomer are joining us from Exeter." Twins! Dark hair, dark eyes, identical smiles. How were we supposed to tell them apart? Maybe we could make one of them get a tattoo.

"Julie Durette, from Hollis. Julie plays a mean second base." Julie grinned; her mouth was filled with red-and-yellow braces—Sting colors.

"Ivy O'Riley, one of the best catchers in the state."

Anyone could see *that* wasn't true. How could that skinny kid jump out of the crouch without tripping over those big feet? And what was with those rubber-band arms? What did the team need this Ivy for, anyway? I was the Sting's number one catcher! And Mac had always told me I was the best catcher in the state.

Unless—

My heart fluttered. Unless Mac was going to let me pitch this year.

"Blair's here," Jess said. A tall girl with shining blond hair approached the field. She wore an expensive wind suit and carried a leather bat bag.

I poked Jess. "You know that girl?"

"I met her some time ago."

I steamed inside but Jess just smiled. Best friends don't keep secrets from each other. As I tried to stare her into apologizing, I noticed that Jess's jaw was twitching, like when an umpire makes a bad call on her pitch but she pretends she didn't notice. That twitch comes from her chewing and swallowing her anger. This was the happiest day of our lives—so what was she angry about?

"So, is she any good?" I whispered.

Jess smiled harder and just shrugged. She was grinding her teeth so hard I could hear it.

"Ladies, I'd like you all to meet Blair Reed," Mac said. His grin was so huge, you'd think he had just won the lottery.

"Um . . . hi," she said.

Jess, Tori, a couple of the new girls said hi back.

"Blair moved here last month from Arizona," Mac

continued. "She'll be doing some pitching for the Sting."

"What?" I felt like I had been punched in the stomach.

Mac shot me a dirty look. "Last year she led her team to the Arizona state championship. They finished eighth at Nationals. Hopefully, we'll have an even better season this year."

Who did Miss Arizona think she was, coming three thousand miles to bounce me out of my only shot at pitching? That settled it—I hated Blair Reed more than I hated anyone in the world.

While I was counting up my list of enemies, I added Ivy and Bridget, too. How could Ivy O'Riley be the best catcher in the state if I was? And what did we need Bridget Ryan for? Maybe I couldn't hit as far as her but I could make my hits count for more. Heck, the slugs in our garden moved faster than Bridget Ryan.

And the clones there, Leigha and Kayleigh—it was going to be a major annoyance, trying to figure out who was who. And who cared, anyway? And who did this Julie think she was, wearing Sting colors on her crooked teeth? *Come back when your teeth are straight!* I wanted to yell.

And Blair Reed with her tanned skin and straight teeth and fancy equipment—I wanted to smack her back to Arizona where she belonged.

Instead, I did the next best thing. "Hey, Blair. Wanna play catch?" I asked.

• • • • •

• • • • •

"Youch!" I cried. Blair almost put the ball through my hand.

"Sorry. I'll take it easy," Blair said.

"No! I just didn't have my glove on right." I whipped the ball back as hard as I could.

A few minutes later, Coach Mac sent the pitchers and catchers to the bullpen to warm up. I lined up with Jess to start her wrist snaps.

"Coach said for Holly to warm me up," Jess said.

"The name is Ivy," the string bean said, snapping her bubble gum. "Only three letters. Sorry if it's too hard for you to remember."

I shuffled over to Blair. "I guess I'm with you again."

"I guess," she said.

Even Blair's wrist snaps had zing to them. *She must have a forearm like a whip,* I thought, finally realizing why Mellissa hounded me to work my snaps.

"So how do you like New Hampshire?" I asked.

"Cold," Blair said, then zinged another ball at me.

"Do you ski?"

"Nope." *Snap-zing.*

"Ice-skate?"

"No ice in southern Arizona." *Snap-zing.*

"We've got some great summer sports up here," I said. "Lots of boating. And hiking, the White Mountains and all that. Ever do any mountain climbing?"

"Nope." *Snap-zing.*

"What about sailing? Or water-skiing?"

"Not a lot of water in Arizona." Blair backed up and began half-throws. *Ka-zing*.

"How about gardening?" I said. "Last year I grew a zucchini the size of a bathtub."

"Really?" Blair stopped, mid-motion.

"Nah," I said. "More the size of my equipment bag. We had to chop it up with an axe to compost it. My father and I grow all sorts of things, but I can't even give them away—my friends hate vegetables."

"Vegetables make me puke," shouted Jenna who had raced over the foul line to catch a long fly.

"Don't mind her," I said. "Everything makes her puke."

"I eat vegetables," Blair said.

"Really? What's your favorite?" I asked.

"None of them. I just eat them because they're good for me."

"So what *do* you like to do?" I asked.

"What do you mean?"

What was with this kid? She had the personality of a paper towel. "I mean—what do you do for fun?"

Blair twirled the ball in her hand, feeling the seams as if they would tell her what to say. "This, I guess."

"This what?" I asked.

"I pitch softball."

Her next toss almost took my head off. I called time, yanked on my mask, and got to work. Or, in Blair's case, fun.

Chapter NINE

Mac divided us into two teams for a little scrimmage. I stayed with Blair as her catcher. We got Nikki, Tori, Julie, and one of the twins. Since I couldn't tell which was Leigha and which was Kayleigh, I called them both Lee-Lee.

The other team had Jess, Ivy, Jenna, Lee-Lee #2, Erin, and Bridget. We were first up so I grabbed my helmet and my bat, ready to do battle with Jess.

Ivy squatted in the catcher's box. She looked like a scarecrow but she snagged Jess's fastball like—well, almost as well as me.

"Strike one!" Mac yelled.

Nikki, coaching third base, yelled, "Keep your eye on the ball, MadCat!"

"Yeah, MudCat," Ivy snorted. " Keep your eye on the

ball. That's the closest you're gonna get to it."

Nikki had signaled *hit away* from the coach's box. I had a better idea—make Ivy work for the title of Best Catcher with the Worst Attitude.

Jess barreled the ball in, low and outside. I laid one down first baseline.

"Bunt!" Jess yelled. Bridget stretched for the throw but I flew through the base.

"Safe!" Mac yelled.

I scratched my nose, the secret sign we had decided on for a steal. I was betting Ivy couldn't gun the ball to second base. Bump and I grew lima beans with more muscle than her.

As soon as Jess's hand windmilled down to her hip, I was off. As I dug for second, Lee-Lee #2 scurried over to cover the base.

I'm no Bridget Ryan—I can outrun any turtle in town, plus a few fat dogs. But the ball was in #2's glove before I even went down for my slide.

I was out by a mile. I glared at Ivy. *I owe you one, Hollyhocks.*

As I plopped on the bench, I was struck with a thought. New girls, new team, new hopes. Even the bench was new to me.

What if this was my new position?

● ● ● ● ●

No one had to run after Bridget's long hits. She didn't have any. Blair struck the Turtle out every time she came up. Blair struck out everyone, except Jess, who beat out a bunt. When she tried to steal second, I fired a throw to Lee-Lee #1, who bobbled it.

Blair's face went hard. She fed Ivy three straight risers. Ivy watched two go by, then tied herself in a knot going for strike three.

I had two hits plus the bunt off Jess that afternoon. I mentally dusted off my spot on the bench and assigned it to Ivy.

The Middlesex College team took over the field at three-thirty. Mac sent us out to wait for our parents. Out in the lobby, things were just plain weird. Leigha and Kayleigh talked but only to each other. Ivy chewed on licorice twists but didn't offer any to the rest of us.

I got dizzy imagining these new girls in Sting uniforms, and Mugger and Casey and the other kids on the wrong side of the fence—the spectator side. I dragged Jess into a corner. "You knew about this, didn't you?"

"They tried to keep it from me. But with Mom as President and all . . ."

"So why didn't you tell me all this stuff was happening?"

"Mom made me promise not to tell anyone," Jess said.

"I'm not just anyone," I protested. "I'm your catcher!"

"This is bigger than just you and me," Jess said.

Jess had the same look on her face that my mom gets when she tells me someday I will appreciate that she made me speak with proper grammar and floss my teeth. I didn't like seeing that look on the face of someone who was supposed to be my best friend.

"What does that mean? Bigger than you and me?"

"It just means that things are going to be different this year. Better."

"For whom?" I asked.

"For all of us, MadCat." Jess squeezed my arm, then ran off after Bridget. Leaving me wondering exactly who *all of us* were.

It sure wasn't the four of our teammates who had been cut, I thought. Then I thought again and realized, yes, it would be different for them, too. While I was playing national-level softball, they might not be playing at all.

● ● ● ● ●

Bump's van was the first to pull up. I almost jumped out of my sneakers when I saw him driving. He had still been in bed when Mom and I had left for practice. I picked up my bat bag, then reached for my equipment bag.

Blair grabbed it, then followed me out to the van. "Is that your dad?" she asked.

"Yeah," I said. "You won't see him very often. He doesn't get to my games." If Blair had half a brain, she'd figure out why from the handicapped plates on the van.

Blair stared up at my father. Bump smiled down at her. He looked pretty good— showered, shaved, with color in his cheeks. Maybe the week in the wheelchair was just a bad spell. MS was like that—good and bad times—maybe Bump would be out in the garden as soon as the ice melted.

"Bump, this is Blair Reed," I said. "She moved here from Arizona."

"Really? Did you just get here? Or were you here for the winter?" Bump asked.

"This isn't winter?" Blair said, her eyes wide.

We both laughed. "Blair, this is my father, Phil Campione."

"Nice to meet you," Blair said.

"You better get back inside," I said. "You'll catch a cold, and Mac will blame me." She waved, then ran back into the lobby.

I reached over and gave Bump a huge hug.

"Come on, Cat," he said, laughing. "You're choking me."

I squeezed him one more time for luck, then fastened the seat belt. Then I saw it—that stupid wheelchair, stacked behind his seat.

MS could be like that, too—from bad to worse.

I looked away, fast.

My teammates were still standing around the lobby, looking weird. Except Blair. She had stayed on the sidewalk. When she saw me look at her, she waved.

She was still waving when we turned the corner.

Chapter TEN

It was Tuesday afternoon of spring vacation. Bump and I were supposed to put in the snow peas but he was still in the recliner at lunchtime. So I went to my second home—the Pages' house.

Jess was making a list of things she wanted to take to Kentucky. "Why do you need seven pairs of socks?" I asked. "The longest we'd be there is four days."

"Like you don't know? Four for me and—"

"I don't always borrow your socks," I said, laughing.

"Oh yeah, that's right!" Jess said, slapping herself on the forehead. "Sometimes you borrow my cleats. Like the time we drove you to the States and you had flip-flops on your feet. You swore your cleats were in your bat bag."

"How was I to know that my mother took them out?"

"To fumigate your bag! Don't you ever wash your catcher's gear?"

"You know the rule," I said. "Nothing gets washed when we're winning."

Jess grinned. "Which means, I'll only need one pair of socks for Nationals, since we're going to win all the games."

"Two pair—one for yourself and one for me in case I forget mine." I stopped laughing, thinking about how much softball lay between us and Nationals. "We aren't going for four months, Jess. And that's only if . . . I mean, *when* . . . we win the National Qualifier."

"Like there's any doubt that we'll win?" Jess said. "With me on the mound, you behind the plate, and Bridget Ryan slamming home runs every other inning? Who's going to beat us?"

"Don't you think it's weird having Bridget and those other kids on our team? We spend all those years trying to beat their butts, and now we have to share the dugout with them?"

"Grow up, MadCat," Jess said. "This isn't about who likes who. It's about who can do what the best."

"So who decided that Blair and Bridget and the others were better than Casey and Mugger and the guys who got cut?"

"The Board of Directors. When the decision was made to go National, they decided to recruit the best players," Jess said. "Not just let a kid on the team 'cuz they had been there the year before."

"So why did we bother with tryouts?" I asked. "None of those girls were even there."

"So no one could say we didn't give them a fair shot," Jess said. "But it was pretty much decided beforehand."

"It's just weird," I said. "I still can't get used to it."

"It's awesome! We're going to be impossible to beat. You saw how good those new kids are."

"Not Ivy," I said, too fast.

"Or Blair," Jess said, just as fast. "Right?"

Jess and I had been friends forever. I wasn't about to let the truth get in the way of that *forever*. "Well, Blair is pretty good," I said. "But anyone can see you're better."

"Yeah, I'm thinking that, too. But it's not a bad idea to work out a little more, especially now basketball is winding down." Jessica Page played soccer in the fall, basketball in the winter, golf in the summer, and softball year-round.

Jess's brothers, Matt and Rick, played football, basketball, and baseball. Their little sister, Emily, danced ballet and tap, and had just joined a gymnastic team. Mr. Page helped coach while Ginny ran the teams and classes from their different Boards.

The Page family wore me out. But I loved them, anyway. I would have liked a brother or sister, but with Bump sick—well, when I needed noise, I was always welcome at Jess's house.

"So what do you want me to do?" I asked.

"What you've always done," Jess said. "Catch for me. Let's do a couple extra sessions a week, okay?"

"Okay," I said. "Let's go practice ourselves to the Nationals."

● ● ● ● ●

We went out to the backyard. Jess blasted rock on the CD player. I did wrist snaps with Jess to warm up. "Hey, you're getting pretty good," Jess said.

I laughed. "Yeah, that's why I gave up five runs in one inning on Saturday."

"So what?" Jess said. "If you keep working, you could be the number two pitcher on the Sting."

"You're kidding, right?"

Jess put her hands on her hips and stared at me. "No, I'm not."

I stopped laughing. Unless I had gone stupid in the past few days, I knew that Jess was going to be the number two pitcher on the Sting. After Blair Reed. I would be a complete jerk to think I could even compete with them in pitching. So I might as well shut up and just catch.

After about an hour, Matt came outside with the portable phone. "Madelyn Catherine, your public is calling."

I nailed him in the head with my glove. He knows I hate my name. Sometimes, when we all go to the mall, he'll have me paged, just to make me crazy.

"Hello?" I growled into the phone.

"MadCat?"

"Yeah?"

"It's Blair. You know, Blair from your team."

I mouthed "Blair" to Jess. She stuck her head on the other side of the receiver.

Blair wanted me to go over to her house. "I can't," I said. "I'm hanging out with Jess." How stupid could this kid be, expecting me to dump Jess and come hang with her?

"She can come, too," Blair said.

Jess put her hand over the mouthpiece. "I have my golf lesson soon. You go."

I stuck the phone against my stomach. "No! A fire hydrant is more fun than her."

"Come on, MadCat." Jess squeezed my arm. "Check her out for me, okay?"

"Nuh-uh." I shook my head. Then I spoke into the phone. "My dad told me not to go anywhere except here."

"My father already talked to your father," Blair said. "He said it was okay."

"He did?" I said. "I mean, I didn't even know my dad knew your dad."

"My father knows everyone—at least in softball."

A man came on the phone. "Hi, MadCat. This is Blair's father, Jim Reed. Your father said it would be okay. I understand your parents have an appointment tonight. So they were happy when I suggested we keep you through suppertime. It should all work out okay."

"Okay," I said. "Sounds like it'll work out."

Jess ran up to change for golf, then waited with me in front of her house. It was late afternoon but still warm. Typical New Hampshire—on Saturday we have summer, on

Monday we have winter, and on Tuesday, spring teases its way back.

After about ten minutes, a big SUV pulled up. It had Arizona plates and a bumper sticker that read:

I HAVE NO LIFE. MY DAUGHTER PLAYS SOFTBALL.

Blair waved at us from the back seat.

Jess waved back. "Check it out and call me when you get home," she said through a huge smile. I could hear that creaking noise—Jess was grinding her teeth again.

The sound stayed with me all the way to Blair's house.

Chapter ELEVEN

Blair Reed lived only a couple of miles away. "So why don't you go to our school?" I asked.

"Blair goes to Nicholls Academy," her father said. "It's supposed to be the best, both academically and athletically."

"They have different vacations than the public schools do," I said.

"They do a lot of things differently than the public schools do," Mr. Reed said.

Blair just looked out the window.

Mr. Reed was the kind of guy you see on television, giving the news. He had a square jaw, clear blue eyes, and dark blond hair. His voice was deep and strong, like he never had a doubt about anything.

Blair looked just like him. But she sounded like she

didn't know anything, at least until someone told her.

Like Blair's school, her house was the best of everything. The game room had leather furniture, a pool table, and a full set of free weights. Her bedroom had cable television, her own phone line, and built-in shelves for her softball trophies.

She even had her own Jacuzzi. "I need it," she said. "My hip gets sore from pitching."

The garage was as big as my house. Half of it housed the cars, lawn mower, snowblower, and the usual outside junk. The other half was a small gym, complete with pull-down basketball hoop, and a collapsible batting cage. A pitching machine leaned against the wall, next to a bucket of balls.

"This is so cool!" I said.

"My father wouldn't take the job in New Hampshire unless I could pitch and hit year-round," Blair said. "My mom found this house. The realtor said it used to belong to a professional wrestler."

"No kidding? Who? Triple Threat? I know he's from around here. Or maybe Indya. She's so cool. She has this move she does—"

"I'm not allowed to watch wrestling," Blair said. "My father says it's not a real sport."

"Never mind," I said. I had forgotten Blair didn't do much for fun.

We shot some baskets for a while. Then Mr. Reed came in. "How about catching Blair for a little bit?" he said.

I had just caught for Jess. During tournament season, I

sometimes catch three games in a day. But it was still spring and my legs felt like rubber bands.

Blair stood under the basket, holding the ball. Waiting for me to answer.

Mr. Reed kept smiling. "It's hard for Blair, coming to a new town, not knowing anyone. I appreciate your coming over."

"I guess I could catch her a little while," I said.

Mr. Reed studied every pitch. He also studied me—my glove position, leg shift, even how I returned the ball. Afterwards, my legs felt like sludge and my arm felt like a wilted dandelion. But Blair seemed happy.

Mrs. Reed made sirloin steak and baked potatoes for supper. I promised to bring her some chives from our herb garden to go with the sour cream. The green beans she served were from a can and tasted like cardboard.

Blair and I sat in the backseat when Mr. Reed drove me home. I was too tired to try to get her to talk. I sat there, trying to figure out why someone who had her own batting cage and Jacuzzi didn't have much to say.

●　●　●　●　●

I stumbled in at seven o'clock that night. I craved a nice salad—those pasty green beans had left a bad taste in my mouth. I planned to squeeze into the recliner with Bump and watch the *Galloping Gardener* on TV.

Mugger sat at our kitchen table, eating zucchini bread. I

had forgotten all about her. "Hey. What's up?" I said.

"Pitching," she said. "You asked me to catch. Tuesdays and Thursdays, remember?"

Talk about old news. My pitching career ended the moment Blair Reed joined the Sting. "Sure," I lied. "Of course I remembered."

It was too dark and cold to throw in the backyard so we went down into the cellar. The good thing about windmill pitching is that the ball is delivered from your hip and the mound is flat. So you don't need the sky over your head to practice pitching, like you do if you pitch baseball.

I could barely walk so I had Mugger do all the wrist snap and arm drills with me. Then I pitched for an hour, taking about ten breaks for water and two more for the bathroom.

I almost jumped for joy when Mr. Murphy appeared at the top of the stairs. "Amanda, let's go," he yelled.

He was already out of the house and in his truck when we got to the back door. I walked Mugger out to the driveway. "Bye," I said. "Thanks."

"See you on Thursday?" she asked.

Thursday was supposed to be the Sting's first outdoor practice. "I'm kind of busy that night. Let's do it another time."

"How about Friday, then?" she said.

We were practicing Friday, too. But Mugger looked so eager, and I felt like such a creep that I said, "Okay. But let's make it really early."

"Okay." Mugger started to walk around the truck.

"Hey, Mugger?" I knew I should say something about her being cut from the Sting.

"Yeah?"

"Never mind," I finally said.

Mugger looked into the truck. Sam Murphy was fiddling with his radio. "Hey, MadCat?"

"Yeah?" I said.

"My father doesn't know yet," she said.

"Know what?" I said, my throat suddenly tight.

"You know what. So don't say anything. All right?"

I nodded, then waved good-bye. I couldn't have said anything if I tried.

Chapter TWELVE

On Friday, my father had an early morning appointment in Boston. He usually saw a doctor in Concord. Going to Massachusetts meant things were bad.

My parents spent Thursday night at Aunt Kay's in Cambridge to avoid rush hour traffic. They asked Mellissa Kubit to stay at our house overnight. When the doorbell rang at seven the next morning, we were still sound asleep.

We got to the door at the same time. Mellissa had a bat in her hand, as if she expected a burglar. But burglars don't ring the doorbell—Muggers do.

"You said early," Mugger said.

"I should have defined 'early,'" I said, yawning.

While Mellissa showered and Mugger watched cartoons, I made French toast. I sliced crusty bread and soaked it in a mixture of eggs and cream, stirred with cinnamon and pure vanilla. I cooked it on a hot griddle and topped it with butter, apple slices, and our own maple syrup.

Mugger polished off four pieces without saying a word.

"If this is how you guys eat breakfast every day, I'm moving in," Mellissa said. After she finished her coffee, she finally seemed to notice Mugger. "Are you on the Sting, too?"

I felt like the biggest jerk in the world.

"No," Mugger said.

After we got the dishes done, Mellissa watched us practice. Our breath frosted in the morning air, but the sky was clear and the sun was warm.

Mugger did the wrist snaps with me like she had the other night. "How long have you been pitching, Mugger?" Mellissa asked.

Mugger shrugged. "I don't pitch."

"Really? You should. You have a super wrist snap. Hey, maybe I should talk to Coach Mac. He's always looking for players with potential."

Mugger dropped her glove, then walked into the house.

"What's that about?" Mellissa asked. "She got something against Mac?"

"More like Mac has something against her." I described how Mugger had been cut after playing for the team for three years, so we could have a National team. "What do you think about that? Is it fair?"

"It depends. If you just want to do something with your

friends, then you keep it local," Mellissa explained. "But if you want to win, you need the best players. And softball's not exactly a cold-weather sport. We're not like California where kids can play it year-round. So around here you might have to go out of town to find enough talent to compete nationally."

Mugger came back out. "Sorry, I had to go to the bathroom," she said. She worked so hard at smiling her gums were showing.

"Hey, Mugger," Mellissa said. "I'm coaching a recreational team this summer. How about you keep working out with MadCat, then you can pitch for me?"

"I don't know," she said. "I'm supposed to be learning to catch. Not pitch." Mugger scratched her head. Her hair was a mass of tangles.

"So you learn catching *and* pitching. What's wrong with that?" Mellissa said.

"Nothing, I guess," Mugger said.

"We'll be starting in late May, when high school ball is over. I'll call you before then, okay? Meanwhile, keep up these drills with MadCat."

"I suppose," Mugger said.

We went on to the arm drills, with Mellissa coaching us both. Each time Mugger made a clean, hard snap, she smiled. A real smile, the kind that mashed her freckles together.

●　●　●　●　●

Mellissa left at ten. She said she'd drop Mugger off on her way to the mall. Mugger got in the front seat and smiled all the way out of the driveway.

Sting practice wasn't until three. It was too nice a day to hang around at home so I called Jess. Her brother Rick said she was at the chiropractor.

"Is she hurt?" I asked.

"Just kind of creaky," Rick said.

Jenna was still in bed. Erin and Tori had gone to an early movie.

Nikki had been grounded for beating up the paper boy. He had tossed the *Times* at their front porch and hit her in the head. She got mad, whipped it back at him, and knocked him off his bike.

I was just about desperate enough to start my homework when the doorbell rang. I ran and opened it, thinking Mugger had come back.

Blair Reed was on my front step.

"Hi," I said.

"Hi," she said. Then she just stood there.

"What're you doing here?" I asked.

"Friday is Personal Development Day at Nicholls," she said. "My father said I should come see you."

"Oh," I said. That kind of made it sound like I had to invite her in.

"Can I see your garden?" Blair asked. I took her out to the patio. "It's all dirt," she said.

"Of course it's dirt. What did you expect?"

"You said you had—those green things for sour cream, you know, for baked potatoes?"

"Chives," I said. "Those are in the herb garden, under a pile of leaves. We haven't uncovered the herbs yet."

"What about the green beans? Where are those?"

"It's too early to put anything in, except for lettuce and snow peas. New Hampshire still has frosts this time of year, sometimes into May. So we start the seeds indoors."

Blair squinted, as if she were trying to imagine an indoor nursery.

"Come on," I said. "I'll show you."

• • • • •

The seedling area in our cellar was three plywood tables under rows of grow-lights.

"Where are the plants?" Blair asked.

Good question. Bump should have started them by now. If we didn't start them this week, we'd have to buy plants at the local superstore.

"I'm supposed to be planting the seeds this morning," I said. "Want to help?"

You would have thought I invited Blair to the moon, she was so excited.

Blair took twice as long as I did with the planting. She looked at each seed carefully like she wanted to make sure it was good enough for her dirt.

Around noon, I had to drag her upstairs for lunch. "But

we have all these seeds left," Blair protested.

"They don't need as early a start," I explained. "Besides, we have to plant the spinach, lettuce, and peas outside before we go to practice."

"Cool," she said. "Let's go do it."

"After lunch," I said. I chopped romaine lettuce, topped it with cold chicken and Mom's homemade Caesar dressing. I toasted the rest of the crusty bread and spread it with cream cheese, then topped it with honey.

Blair looked cross-eyed at her plate. "If you don't eat, you can't plant," I said. After only four days, I already knew that Blair liked being told what to do.

By the time I had poured our milk, Blair was halfway through the salad and reaching for her toast.

"Let's eat fast," she said. "I can't wait to plant in the real garden."

Cripes. I was going to be stuck with this kid for the whole growing season. I supposed that was okay—until Bump got out of that stupid wheelchair, I would need the help.

Blair Reed wasn't exactly who I would have recruited for the job. But I guess she was on the team, whether I wanted her there or not.

Chapter
THIRTEEN

We were just *so* good.

Every girl on the team threw like a rocket, fielded like a vacuum cleaner, and ran like the wind. Well—except for Bridget Ryan, who moved only slightly faster than the broken bulldozer in Mugger's backyard.

Coach Mac looked twenty years younger, smiling as he put us through throwing and fielding drills.

The sky was crystal-blue with an occasional cloud stretched high and long. The infield was mushy in spots from the weekend's ice storm but the outfield was the lime green of spring grass.

After an hour of drills, Mac sent us to position practice. Blair and Jess went to the sidelines to pitch with Mr. Reed. Jess had her arm around Blair like they were best friends. It gave me the creeps, watching Jess act friendly to someone I knew she didn't much like.

Maybe she was putting the team ahead of her personal feelings. I hoped that was all it was, but these days I couldn't even guess at what Jess was thinking a lot of the time.

Ginny took four kids into the batting cage, which left six of us in the infield. Blair and Jess kept pitching.

Lee-Lee, Bridget, Erin, and Nikki would be doing base and running duty while Ivy and I practiced our throws to the bases.

"Want to go first?" I asked Ivy.

"Sure. Why not?" She got down into her crouch, with her sharp knees almost in her ears.

Ivy made twenty throws. Erin made it safe to second base once. Nikki stole safely three times. Sixteen outs from twenty steal attempts was pretty good.

I tightened my shinpads, thinking how stupid I was to worry about getting a pitching slot when I was going to have to work my butt off to keep my own position as catcher.

Mac motioned me into the box. Nikki switched with Bridget so Bridget could practice running.

"Time!" I yelled. I ran over to Lee-Lee. "Nice work." She had made every tag, never bobbling the ball.

"Thanks."

"You're Kayleigh, right?"

"Leigha."

"Jeepers! How am I supposed to tell you apart?" They

63

were the same height, with shoulder-length black hair, dark skin, and big eyes.

Leigha pointed to a tiny birthmark on the left side of her jaw.

"That's it?" I said. "The only difference?"

"That, and I dress better," Leigha said. "Kayleigh is a clunker. I'm the cool one."

"Okay, I got it." I hustled back to the catcher's box, trying to memorize the birthmark since I couldn't tell the difference between being a clunker and being cool.

Erin and Bridget alternated running. I took ten throws, nailing each one. Then Ivy yelled "Time!"

Ivy dragged me out to Mac. "No offense to Ryan-the-Rocket," she whispered, "but this is like shooting fish in a toilet."

"What the heck do you mean?" Mac asked.

"Bridget can't run for beans," Ivy said. "MadCut could probably walk the ball to second base and get her out."

"MadCat!" I yelped.

"Yeah. Whatever," Ivy said. "Let me run."

Mac looked at me. "Let her," I said. "We'll still get the out."

Ivy grabbed a helmet, went to first, and got into her runner's stance. At shortstop, Leigha wrinkled her face at me as if to say, *Is this kid just too lame or what?*

I crouched down and signaled for the pitch. Mac threw a changeup! Ivy could have somersaulted to second in the time it took the ball to reach me. When the ball finally hit my mitt, I whipped it with all my might.

Leigha made a perfect tag. Ivy was out by half an inch—but she was out.

"Way to cover, Leigha-lee," I shouted, trying not to dance.

"You got lucky. You can't do it again," Ivy said, heading back for first base.

"I can do it all day," I yelled.

And we did, ten more times. I was really good. But Leigha did all the damage. Wherever I threw the ball—a bit low, a bit wide, a bit high—Leigha snagged it and got down for the tag.

"Enough," Mac said.

"No!" Ivy's legs were shaking. "I can beat her, I know I can!"

"I said, that's enough. I need a break!" Mac looked over at the Porta Potties. He had already downed two ice coffees and practice was only half over.

"I'll take over," Mr. Reed piped up. Jess and Blair had stopped their drills to watch Ivy and me duel over second base.

Mac glared at him. "These girls need to sit down. They're hot."

"They're hot to compete," Mr. Reed said, glaring back. "We'd be fools to stop that."

Ginny Page walked over to Mr. Reed. She didn't say a word; she just stood next to him and stared at Mac.

Mac tossed Mr. Reed the ball, and headed off the field.

He looked old again, his shoulders slumping.

Mr. Reed whispered something to Ivy. Her sweat-soaked face broke into a bright smile. Then he patted her shoulder and went to the pitcher's rubber.

Mr. Reed snapped a fastball, right down the middle of the plate. *Easy out*, I thought.

Leigha smiled as I whipped the ball to her. *Easy out.* She snagged the ball, then went down for the tag. Ivy was four strides off the bag, caught dead.

It was like watching a movie in slow motion, each moment unfolding in a long, clear picture.

Ivy bent like a charging bull.

Leigha realizing that Ivy hadn't gone down for a slide.

Leigha turning her head and tucking into her shoulder.

Ivy finally going down, too late!

Leigha airborne, sunlight between her and the ground.

Ivy flopping over the base.

The ball rolling into center field.

Then everything got fast, really fast. Mr. Reed yelling, "Make the play!" Nikki running to Leigha instead of to the ball. Ivy now running to third. Erin charging the ball and whipping a long one home, where I was waiting.

If Ivy tried to knock me down, I would slap that tag right on her ugly face. But Ivy slid under me before I could get the ball down.

"Safe!" Mr. Reid yelled.

The field went dead quiet. The only sound was the whir of the pitching machine and Ivy's hard panting.

Mr. Reed gave Leigha the thumbs-up. She was okay but looked like she'd like to body-block him to the parking lot.

Coach Mac started for the field. Ginny put out her hand to stop him. "Listen up, girls!" she called. "Mr. Reed has something to explain to you."

Mr. Reed turned in a slow circle, to make sure all of us were listening. Then he spoke to us in that loud and confident voice.

"That, my dear ladies, is how you play to win."

STING INVITED TO NFS WORLD SERIES QUALIFIER

The Northeast Sting travel to Lowell, Massachusetts, this weekend to participate in the National Fastpitch Softball Qualifier. The Sting, based out of Norwich, New Hampshire, earned the opportunity to compete in the Qualifier based on their three first-place tournament wins this June.

The winning team of each age division in the Qualifier will travel to the World Series in Louisville, Kentucky, which brings together more than six hundred teams to compete for National titles in age groups from 10U through 18U.

"The girls have worked tremendously hard," says Judd MacMahon, Sting coach. "We set a goal this April and we did our . . .

Chapter FOURTEEN

I hurt so much, I could cry.

"It's okay to cry," Mom would say. "Everyone cries."

"Focus, MadCat," Coach MacMahon would growl. Except Mac didn't say much these days—Mr. Reed and Ginny did most of the talking for the team.

The new Sting had been together for more than two months. In that time we had practiced our butts off, gotten to know one another, and won the three tournaments we had entered.

All of it was only preparation for the National Qualifier in Lowell, Massachusetts. There were more than a hundred and fifty teams here this weekend, from all over New England. The winning teams in each age division got a trophy as big as me and a berth to Kentucky, to play in the NFS World Series.

"You okay?" Jess whispered behind her glove.

"That foul tip—look!" I showed Jess a lump the size of an egg under my kneepad.

"Gross," she said. "You gonna sub out?"

"Are you nuts?" I said.

"Are *you* nuts?" Jess echoed. "What if your knee is broken?"

"If it was broken, I'd be rolling on the ground, throwing up," I said. "Besides, would you sub out?"

Jess looked out to center field where Blair Reed was snapping an imaginary ball into her glove. "No way."

"Ditto that." I handed Jess the ball. "Now let's get this hookworm out."

We had won our first game today, against a team from Rhode Island. Bridget hit two home runs and Blair had shut them out, 12–zip. The game was ended in the fifth inning by the "mercy rule" because we were ahead by more than ten runs. I had an easy game behind home plate—not one ball in the dirt, not one ball to the backstop.

I had assumed Ivy would catch this game. In our earlier tournaments we had alternated as catcher, just like Blair and Jess had alternated as pitcher. But when Mac was making out the lineup, Ginny got in his ear.

By the time he posted the lineup, I was catcher and Ivy was in right field. And here I would stay, even if my knee was swelling like a cantaloupe. I had learned an important lesson when the Sting Board of Directors cut Mugger and the other girls. *Anyone* can be replaced, even someone who's been on the team forever. Mugger was playing on Mellissa's rec team, I knew, but what were Ashley, Casey, and Nina doing this weekend? Did they go nuts every Friday afternoon, wanting to pack their bat bags for the weekend tournament that they no longer got to go to?

No time to worry about that now. They were there, I was here, and I was here to play. It was the bottom of the seventh inning. Even though we were ahead, 2–zip, the Connecticut Cardinals had been pounding the stuffing out of Jess for the whole game. Ivy, Jenna, and Blair were running like dogs in the outfield, taking down long flies.

We needed to shut down the Cardinals this inning and win the game.

"Throw hard!" Ginny Page yelled.

Jess pitched and—*BAM!* The batter crushed the ball to right field for a long single.

Jess walked the next batter. Two on, no outs. A home run would kill us. "Throw hard, Jess," I called. "You can do it."

Jess rubbed her eyes, as if she was wiping away tears. I called time and ran out to her. "You okay?"

"I am throwing hard," she said. "Why is everyone telling me to throw hard?" Jess stared into the dugout at her mother.

"It's just what people say. It doesn't mean anything."

"Then they ought to shut up about it," she said.

"It's just like when people say 'keep your eye on the ball.' I mean, think how stupid that would be, if this goober really kept her eye *on* the ball," I said.

Jess looked me like I had an eggplant for a nose.

"As a catcher," I continued, "I refuse to catch any ball with an eye sitting on top of it. Like, how gross can you get?"

Jess laughed. "You are so insane, MadCat."

"Which is why no one dares to call me Madelyn."

Jess was still laughing as she struck out the next batter. But she stopped after she walked the next batter. Bases loaded, one out. Jess rubbed the ball hard, like she was trying to push some strikes into it.

Jess wound up and threw. YOUCH! The ball hit the batter on the foot. She took first base, forcing the Cardinals' first run to score.

One out. The score was now 2–1, with a Cardinal runner on every base. Ginny Page shook the dugout fence. "Throw hard!"

Jess whipped the ball, hard but low. *Ball one,* I thought but the batter went for it. A little squibbler, spinning in the dust in front of the plate.

I jumped on it. All the runners were flying but the only runner I was concerned with was almost on my face—the girl charging in from third.

The tying run!

Somehow I flipped backwards onto my butt—and home plate. The runner tripped over me but I held the ball.

"Out!" the umpire yelled.

Two outs. Bases still loaded. A walk would tie the game. A hit would probably win it.

Jess threw three balls in a row. She was one bad pitch from tying the game.

In the dugout, Ginny Page and Mr. Reed had Mac surrounded. Ginny wanted Jess to stay in; Mr. Reed wanted to bring Blair in as a reliever. All three of them were red-faced.

Just as I settled into my crouch, Mac headed out to Jess. He said something to her, then he motioned to center field. *Mr. Reed won that one,* I guessed.

Blair ran in. Jess walked slowly out to center field. The fans for both teams applauded but Jess kept her eyes on the ground, probably wishing she were a grub so she could burrow in and hide herself. It's hard enough to be lifted for another pitcher but to be taken out in the middle of a count is absolutely humiliating.

After Blair took five warm-up pitches, the batter stood back in at the plate. Still three balls, no strikes. Blair's first pitch was a soft strike. The batter slammed it foul.

Blair threw again, this time a sizzler. The batter didn't even lift her bat. "Stee-r-r-r-ike two!" the umpire yelled.

Blair's face showed nothing. She wound up and—

The batter was just starting her swing as the ball hit my glove. "Stee-r-r-r-ike three!"

The Sting side went nuts. Julie whirled Leigha around, then tried to pick Bridget up. Erin was shaking me, then before I knew it, I was twirling Ivy in a happy circle.

Jess pushed through the celebration and gave Blair a hug. "Way to win the game," Jess said.

"The *W* goes in the book under your name," Blair said. "I just did a little cleanup."

We all headed for home plate to shake hands with the

Cardinals. "The *S* goes under Blair's name," Jess whispered in my ear.

"Huh?" I said.

"*S* for show-off," Jess said. Then she smiled, said "Nice job," and slapped hands with all the Cardinals. "Good game, good game, good game," the Connecticut girls answered one after another, though not one of them meant it.

I didn't blame them. It didn't feel like a good game to me either.

And I was the winner.

Chapter FIFTEEN

"Geronimo!" I screamed and flung myself into space.

Ivy disappeared under an avalanche of water. She appeared a minute later, splashing and sputtering.

It was a hot June night, stuffy enough to make me sweat even though I was in shorts and a T-shirt instead of my catcher's gear. Even so, it was an awesome night—we were celebrating three straight wins in the Qualifier.

Blair had pitched the last game of the day, another shutout. I had caught while Ivy played right field. We scored four runs. Bridget drove in three and I drove in one, with a solo home run.

Our first game wasn't until noon tomorrow so the Reeds invited the team and their families to their house. Everyone went nuts when they saw the pool, with its diving board, loop-de-loop slide, and attached hot tub. Ivy didn't even bother to change—she jumped in wearing her uniform.

"Just get wet," Mr. Reed nagged. "Nothing strenuous."

Bump sat in a lawn chair and talked to Julie's parents. Even though he didn't make it to the games, Mom made him come to the picnic to meet all the parents. He had hobbled to the backyard with his cane, his bad leg dragging. It had taken him forever, but that Campione pride had kept him from taking his wheelchair.

Right before dark, Mr. Reed ordered us out of the pool. We all groaned. "You kids get changed and play in the backyard for a little while," Ginny Page said. "The parents need to talk."

I was near the end of the line for the pool house, with five girls ahead of me. The water dripping off my hair and down my back made me want to pee—right then and there.

"Can I cut?" I moaned. "I gotta go bad." Julie stepped aside. Jess waved me forward.

Ivy blocked me. "If I have to wait my turn, you have to wait yours, MuttCat."

"Come on," I whined. "Let me cut."

Ivy leaned really close and whispered, "Maybe Coach can take my place away from me. But you can't."

Bump said giving people the finger causes more fights than anything he knows. But I had to hold my hand down to keep from flipping my middle finger in Ivy's face— maybe right up her nose!

Instead, I ran into the house. The guest bathroom was down the hall from the living room so I could hear all the parents talking at once. Then some woman with a raspy voice yelled, "I didn't let my kid join this team so she could sit on the bench!" Mac mumbled something, then people were trying to out-shout each other.

I waited another minute, straining to listen. When I didn't hear Mom's or Bump's voice, I stepped into the bathroom. Whatever the problem was, they were silent.

Which meant I was okay.

●　●　●　●　●

The moon was full and high, outshining a billion bright stars. Patches of silver speckled the yard with magic light and soft shadows. The peepers chirped and the fireflies flashed.

No one had come out to take us home or tell us we could go inside. So we did the only logical thing—we played hide-and-seek.

Jess's brothers, Rick and Matt, volunteered to be "It." They boasted they could find all twelve of us in less than ten minutes. Julie and Tori had been making girlie-eyes at Rick and Matt all night and were guaranteed to be the first ones found.

Most of my teammates ran around like Barbie dolls with their brains removed. They had no clue where to hide. I ran for the east side of the yard. There was a big maple tree out there, hidden by some white pines that hadn't been clipped in years.

The leaves blocked most of the moonlight, so it took a

few seconds to realize I wasn't the only monkey climbing the tree. "Who's there?" I said, panting hard.

"The boogeyman! Now get lost before I rip your head off and toss it to a skunk."

"Ivy! Get out! I was here first," I said, not entirely sure that I had been.

"Some jock you are," Ivy said. "You're about to have cardiac arrest."

"Shut up. I'm as good as you," I said.

"You're better than me!" Ivy whispered. "But only at kissing butt."

"What? I am not a butt-kisser!"

"Then why do you get most of the starts as catcher?"

"I don't!" I whispered myself hoarse. "We trade off."

"Now there's a fair trade-off! Blair starts the first game of every day," Ivy said. "So Blair pitches Friday night. Blair pitches Saturday morning, then Jess. Then Blair starts first game Sunday, then Jess. So Her Queenship ends up pitching almost twice as much as Jess. And since you're Her Majesty's preferred catcher, you catch twice as much as me."

"Who says I'm Her Maj—Blair's—favorite catcher?"

"Her bigmouthed father," Ivy said. "Didn't you notice? That goon hangs on Mac like snot every time Mac makes up the lineup."

"No. I did not notice," I said. But the truth was, I had. I just didn't have any complaints.

"Then today, Mrs. Big-shot President throws a fit," Ivy continued. "She thinks Jess—the Crown Princess—pitches better if you catch, so you get that game, too. It worked, hanging out at their houses. Kissing coach butt."

"I'm not kissing butt, you jerk-face," I said. "I'm just being friends. You could hang out, if you wanted."

"Really? How am I supposed to get here?"

"Like I do," I said. "Ride your bike."

"Twelve miles north from Nashua?"

"Oh," I said.

"Oh," Ivy mocked. "Answer me this, Campione. If they weren't going to play me, why did they recruit me?"

"Who recruited you?" *I sure as heck didn't,* I thought.

"Mrs. Page, first. My mother said, no, I should be playing in Nashua with my own friends. Then Coach Mac and Mr. Reed came down, told my mom and me that I'd have a better shot at making the high school team if I played on a National-level tournament team."

"That's nuts. You're a good player. You'd make the high school team," I said.

"Maybe in a cow town like Norwich," Ivy said. "But in Nashua, we have one public high school for three thousand kids. You gotta be freaking awesome to make the varsity in a school that big. No varsity means no college scholarship."

"I never thought about that," I said.

"Why should you? Nikki said you'll get to go to the University of New Hampshire free because your father is a cripple."

"Shut up!" I said. I grabbed a handful of leaves and twisted, wishing it was Ivy's scrawny neck.

"At least you've got a father," Ivy said. "If I want to go to college, I have to get a scholarship. Which is why my mother and some others are pissed off about our playing time."

"Everyone gets to play," I said. "We're fair."

"Think about it, MadCat. Really think about it, then tell me this is a fair team."

Chapter SIXTEEN

The trick to winning at hide-and-seek is keeping completely quiet. But that's not why Ivy and I sat in that tree in total silence for ten minutes.

I had a lot of thinking to do. Was the Sting a *fair* team? And what exactly did *fair* mean?

Was it *fair* that four of my old teammates got cut? It was for the good of the team, Ginny Page had said, to make the team stronger. But what good did it do to make a team stronger if you weren't on the team anymore?

What about the kids who were on the team? I had played every minute of every game today. Blair and Jess had, too. Kayleigh didn't get to bat, even though she played the field. Bridget was in two games as the designated hitter; she only got in the field once.

Erin hadn't really played much at all. Sure, she pinch-ran for a couple of kids but that was it. But you couldn't take out an awesome fielder like Leigha at shortstop to let Erin play. Could you? Wasn't that what it was about, this *going National* business? Putting the best team on the field?

"Are we supposed to be playing fair?" I finally said. "Or playing to win?"

The silence was so long and so deep, I thought Ivy had slipped out of the tree. Then, in a quiet voice, she answered me. "Can't we do both?"

Someone pushed through the pines, running right under us. "Madelyn Catherine, come out this minute!" Matt called.

Ivy's eyes went wide. She mouthed, "Madelyn Catherine?" I shook my fist. Ivy puffed her cheeks like a chipmunk, trying to swallow her giggles. I almost fell out of the tree, trying to keep the laughter in my belly.

Finally Ivy leaned her face against the trunk of the tree, and sighed.

"We won about fifteen minutes ago," I whispered. "Want to get down?"

"In a minute," Ivy said. She pushed aside a branch and looked out into the night. The sky was a deep blue and seemed to go on forever.

"It's nice to get see the moon without anything getting in the way," she said. "In downtown Nashua, it never really gets dark, not with all the buildings and streetlights."

"If you say so," I said.

"Think I'm weird?"

"Absolutely," I said.

"Figures," she snapped. She slipped down about three branches.

I hooked my knees over the limb and swung upside down so I was face-to-face with her. "I like weird," I said.

"No, you don't."

"Yes. I do. Weird is good," I swore.

A breeze picked up, making the leaves dance with silver light. I grinned an upside-down smile.

Ivy grinned back. "Okay. Let's go inform those dork-balls that you and I have won this game," she said.

The other kids had given up hide-and-seek and were tossing water balloons at one another. I stopped Ivy before she opened the gate to the pool deck. "You never said what you thought. Are we supposed to worry about being fair?" I asked. "Or about winning?"

Ivy shrugged. "All I know is that being fair but not winning kind of stinks. But winning and not being fair stinks more."

• • • • •

"What were you guys talking about all this time?" I asked. It was almost eleven and we were just heading home.

"Coach Mac won't be coaching the Sting anymore," Bump said.

"What!" I almost ripped out of my seat belt.

Mom sighed. "Pansy, he's been—"

Bump cut her off. "He's been at it too long, is what he told us."

"Phil," Mom said. "That's not—"

"Let it go, Anita," Bump barked.

"Let what go?" I asked.

"Mac. The guy is over sixty," Bump said. "His wife is retired. He needs to be at home."

"He never worried about that before," I whined.

"Things change, Cat. Deal with it," Bump snapped.

"What is your problem?" I snapped back.

"Nothing!" Bump said. "Everything. The only thing I've got the energy to do is be miserable." In the moonlight, his face sagged. "I'm sorry, Cat."

"No, I'm sorry," I said. "I'm glad you came to the party."

Bump leaned his head back. "Me, too."

"Madelyn, are you okay with how things have been going with your team?" Mom asked.

"I suppose so," I said. "Maybe it stunk that Mugger and them got cut. But, if we're going National—I mean, look at Leigha. We need players like her. Nothing gets by that kid."

"No, nothing does. She's a nice girl, too. They all seem to be. But what I meant is—you're all being expected to play . . ." Mom's voice tapered off.

"Harder," Bump said. "Tougher. Are you doing okay with that, Cat?"

"Why do you keep asking that? Did someone say I wasn't?" I said, suddenly panicked. "Like I'm not hustling enough? Or good enough?"

"Of course not," Bump said. "We just want to make sure that you're managing with the changes. They're more . . . " Now his voice tapered off.

"Dramatic," my mother concluded. "Far more than we expected."

Mom turned the car into the driveway. Suddenly I was too bone-tired to even lift a finger, let alone have a *dramatic* conversation.

"We're more than fine," I said. "We're the best. That's what we're supposed to be. Right?"

"I'm just not sure," Mom said.

"Well, we are!" I jumped out of the car. "And we'll prove it tomorrow when we win the National Qualifier."

Chapter SEVENTEEN

We were slimy with sweat, coated with dirt, and stinking like an umpire's coffee breath. But we were golden.

It was four o'clock on Sunday afternoon. We were still undefeated in the National Qualifier. We had won the quarterfinal game at noon, and had just slammed a Maine team in the semifinals.

Twenty teams in the 12U division had started on Friday night, and it was down to this—the Northeast Sting and the Central Massachusetts Terminators. We would be playing at six PM for the championship and for a berth to the NFS World Series in Kentucky.

Mr. Reed had taken over the coaching duties, with Mrs. Page and the twins' mom, Mrs. Loomer, as assistants. It didn't take a genius to figure out that Ginny was trying to keep the Norwich and out-of-town parents happy by balancing the coaching. It seemed to work out okay—we were still winning.

Mr. Reed ordered us to sit in the shade, eat, and rest until it was time to start pregame warm-up. I found a nice grassy spot, then looked for Jess. She was across the field, heading for the parking lot, deep in conversation with Blair Reed.

"Hey, Jess!" I bellowed.

She turned and looked, puzzled.

"Over here!" I pointed down at the blanket Mom had given me.

Jess shrugged, then turned and kept walking.

"Her Majesty and the Crown Princess are being whisked away in their royal carriage," Ivy said. "Off to the mall."

"Huh?" I said. "Oh, I get it. You mean 'ball.'"

"You heard what I said." Ivy shook her head like I was the densest turnip on earth, then sat down with her lunch.

I watched Jess and Blair as they climbed into Mr. Reed's big SUV. "They're going to the mall so they can be in air-conditioning for a while," Nikki whispered. "Being as how they're the two pitchers and all."

I sat down and shoved off my cleats. My feet stunk because I was keeping to the rule—no changing socks until the team lost. For the past three years, and even this year, Jess and I ran a suppertime contest over whose feet stunk worse. Whoever was brave enough to be judge got extra bubble gum. Yesterday Kayleigh had won.

"Want to go up against my feet?" Nikki said.

"No, that's all right. I'd win, hands down," I said, trying to sound confident. I pulled off my socks. They were stiff in my hands because we hadn't lost since mid-June, one meaningless game in the middle of a round-robin tournament.

It wasn't until now that I remembered Jess pulling clean socks out of her bag and putting them on before the last game. She had broken the rule and changed her socks, without even consulting me on it.

Mom touched my shoulder. "Tulip, you need to eat something."

"I'm not that hungry."

"Of course you are." She handed me a plastic bowl filled with greens from our garden—spinach, lettuce, pea pods. The salad was topped with roast lamb, feta cheese, and our own red-wine vinaigrette.

Suddenly I was hungry.

"Gross! How can you eat that stuff?" Jenna stuffed her face with a sausage sub topped with onions.

"It's awesome," I said, gnawing on a pea pod. There was something about crisp vegetables that made me feel fresh, even though I alone was keeping up with the stinky socks rule.

"Hey, I like salad," said Tori. "But only with that other lettuce, that white stuff."

"Iceberg lettuce?" I said. "You might as well eat paper. Green leaf and romaine lettuce have vitamins and fiber. Spinach has iron."

"Like I said—gross!" Jenna sneered. Tori high-fived her.

Ivy poked me. "Hey, Ragweed. Can I have some of that?"

"You don't mind getting poisoned?" I said.

"Better than getting a heart attack," she said, staring at Jenna. "You know how much fat is in that crap?"

"Not enough!" Jenna sputtered. Tori high-fived her again.

I passed Ivy a fork and she dug in with me. "Hey. Good game this morning," I said. Ivy had caught while Jess pitched a 2–0 shutout.

"Yeah, you too," she said.

We had won the second game, 3–1. Blair had pitched a no-hitter. The run came on a walk, then a steal. The runner was incredibly fast but I had her gunned down at third—until Kayleigh bobbled the ball. It corkscrewed into the other team's dugout and the runner was awarded home.

Mr. Reed didn't say a word. He just stared at Kayleigh as if he wanted to squeeze her so tight, she'd never bobble another ball.

Ivy cleared her plate. I split my carrot cake with her. It was so sweet and spicy, I almost drooled down my shirt.

I laid back down, my stomach full. The sun was lower now, coming in under the leaves instead of through them. It felt good on the side of my face.

Suddenly a shadow crossed over me. I opened my eyes. Ginny Page stood in the middle of our circle. "Girls," she said. "You'll all have to come with me. We have a problem."

• • • • •

The Terminators' coach had challenged our roster. That meant that the Tournament Director had to check each player on the team to verify that we were all legal. One by one, we had to go into the concession stand and meet with the Director.

"Madelyn Campione?" she called.

Mom and I stepped in.

Ginny Page stood behind the Director. Next to her was a big man with a shiny bald head and mean eyes. He wore a purple shirt, monogrammed with the Terminators' logo— a wolf.

"Date of birth?" the Director asked. I told her. She looked at my birth certificate, then checked the birth date listed on the roster.

"Address?" she asked. I told her. I felt shaky, like I had been called in front of my math class to do a problem I couldn't solve in a million years.

"Can I see your driver's license?" the Director asked my mother.

"Of course," Mom said, taking out her wallet. "May I ask why?"

"The proofs-of-residence for the Norwich girls are apparently not sufficient," the Director said.

"This is ridiculous," Ginny snapped. "We've been using report cards for years. The Commissioner always accepted them."

The Terminators' coach poked his finger on the roster. His sunburned head reminded me of a beefsteak tomato. "This is for Nationals," Beefsteak said. "Without a town and state on the report cards, this Nissitissit Middle School could be in Kansas, for all I know. You have to prove conclusively that your girls all reside in the New England conference."

"You know darn well who these kids are," Ginny snapped. "We've been playing you for years."

"This isn't the Sting team I know," he snapped back. "Where's that kid with all the freckles? What was her name? Slugger what's-her-name?"

"Mugger," I said automatically.

"And that girl with the red goggles? Casey."

I felt queasy. I hadn't thought much about Casey all weekend, or Nina and Ashley. Mugger and I pitched together every week but I never thought about her and the Sting in the same space in my brain. And yet, like a ladybug on the underside of a lettuce leaf, my old teammates crawled around on the undersides of my thoughts.

Ladybugs were garden friends, not pests. Mugger, Nina, Ashley, and Casey had been summer friends and good players. Maybe not as good as the team I was on now but we'd had eaten a lot of dirt and won a lot of games back on the old Sting.

But the old Sting wouldn't win this National Qualifier. This year's team would, when we got past the

93

Terminators and Coach Beefsteak.

"We've made some changes this year," Ginny said, her voice cold.

"No kidding," Beefsteak said. "You brought in a ringer from Arizona."

"The Reed girl is legal," the Director said. "All her paperwork is in order."

"But six of these girls are not," he said, this time to the Director. "If you were doing your job, you would have caught this Friday night."

I felt like I was going to throw up, right on the Beefsteak's smelly feet. But then he'd try to disqualify me for puking in public.

"Don't worry, Madelyn," the Director said. "The Commissioner said we can verify you if your parents can prove their residency."

She looked at Mom's driver's license, then checked it against our address listed on the roster. "Okay, you're set," she said. "See, wasn't that easy?"

I went outside, holding my stomach. "I think I'm gonna have diarrhea," I mumbled.

"Don't let that jerk get to you." Mr. Reed put his hand on my shoulder. "It's a cheap trick. Get the other team riled before the big game. We'll be fine. You'll see."

"I don't feel fine," I said.

Mr. Reed leaned close to me and smiled. The sun was behind him, making his blond hair match the fire in his eyes. At that moment I would have believed him if he told me I could do a backflip over the dugout. "That's because that jerk was messing with your head. But think of this, MadCat: We're gonna beat his sorry butt so far into the ground that he'll look up and see China."

Chapter EIGHTEEN

We weren't fine. In fact, we were in a royal mess. *Buried under a load of manure without a shovel*, Bump would say.

The only Nissitissit Middle School kids we could verify were Jess and me. The other Norwich parents weren't at the field to show their driver's licenses.

Erin's parents had driven into Boston because her mother was flying out on a business trip. Tori's family had rushed home so her mom could get the baby to bed. Tori's dad had been on his way back to Lowell when his car broke down. Nikki's parents went to pick him up.

Jenna's sister had an ice-hockey practice so her mother drove her and Jenna's dad north to Norwich, then headed back for the big game. Jenna said her mother hated highways and was probably coming south from New Hampshire on old Route 3—the long, slow way to Lowell.

The Tournament Director yelled at Coach Beefsteak. "We all know these girls are legal! You're trying to win the Qualifier on a technicality."

"No, I'm trying to play by the rules. I had to run all over Worcester County, getting my proofs-of-residency. Why should the Sting get off easy?" he said. "Besides, it's not my fault if you were sloppy when you approved their roster."

The Northeast Sting had to play the game with only eight players. Even if we won, we still had to verify the residencies of Erin, Tori, Jenna, and Nikki by the time the Qualifier was over. If their parents weren't rounded up by then, we'd forfeit the whole tournament because the *disqualified* girls had played in all the other games.

Nikki kicked the ground while Erin, Tori, and Jenna sobbed. Mom tried to hug them all at once but they wouldn't be comforted.

"You're still part of this team," Mr. Reed bellowed at them. "Act like it!"

They wiped their tears, then climbed the backstop to cheer us through warm-ups.

The rest of us took the field. The starting lineup looked like this:

Ivy	right center field	**Blair**	pitcher
Jess	left center field	**Leigha**	shortstop
MadCat	catcher	**Julie**	second base
Bridget	first base	**Kayleigh**	third base

Ivy stared at the lineup like she wanted to rip it to shreds. "I'm sorry," I said. "It's kind of your turn to catch."

"Forget it," she said. "With only two outfielders, the team needs my speed out there."

I grabbed Kayleigh as she left the dugout. "What?" she said.

I wanted to tell her to squeeze her glove on my throws to third. She wouldn't have a left fielder backing her up if she bobbled the ball.

"What?" she said again. Leigha was right—Kayleigh was a clunker, with her hair sticking out of her cap and ketchup on her chin.

But she was *our* clunker. "You're gonna do great," I said. I fixed her hat, then pushed her out to the field. I left the ketchup—maybe it would scare the Terminators.

As I snapped on my shinpads, I watched Mrs. Loomer warm up Blair. Everything about her was long and strong. And that wrist snap! Her arm slowly windmilling up, then gaining speed on the downswing until *WHIP!* The ball shot out at her hip like a missile.

Blair Reed made any catcher look darn good. I was happy to be along for the ride. I just hoped Her Majesty was strong enough to take us all the way to Kentucky.

•   •   •   •   •

Our good-luck charm, Bridget Ryan, won the coin toss. We chose to be home team so we could get the last at-bats. Blair struck out the side on ten pitches in the top of the first. Then we got up.

The Terminators' pitcher was huge, the size of a high school basketball player. Her hair was dyed the same color as her sunburned face—a cheap pink.

"Mr. Reed should have demanded to see that hambone's birth certificate," I complained.

"He did," Jess said.

Hambone's control wasn't great but she threw hard. After fouling about eight in a row, Ivy drew a walk.

Jess was too hungry for a hit. She struck out on a ball at her ankles. I passed her as she stormed back to the dugout. She let out a string of words I didn't even realize she knew, let alone would say.

"Hey," I said. "It's not the end of the world."

Jess stopped cold and stared at me. Her face was so angry, for a crazy moment I thought she was going to swing the bat at me. "Get real, MadCat," she hissed.

I stepped up to the plate, thinking that the pain in my knee, the dirt on my face, and the sweat in my shoes was about as real as could be. I didn't know what Jess's problem was but I knew better than to let it get in my head while I was at bat.

Mr. Reed, coaching at first, gave me the *take* sign so Ivy could steal. The pitcher began her motion. I faked a bunt. Ivy jumped off first.

Too early, I thought.

The pitch was at my shoulders. "Ball one," the umpire called.

The base umpire jerked his right hand over his head. "Runner is OUT. She left the base too early." The rule was that the runner couldn't leave the base until the ball left the pitcher's hand.

"What? Are you nuts?" Ivy screamed.

Mr. Reed got in the ump's face. "I was right there, Blue! She left on time. Not early."

Why was Mr. Reed arguing? Either he was blind or lying—even though I was at bat, I caught Ivy leaving early.

I steered Ivy toward our dugout before she punched someone out. "Freaking idiot," she snarled.

"The umpire?" I said.

"That moron Reed," Ivy snapped. "He said that the base umpire wasn't paying attention so I should leave as soon as the pitcher started her delivery." Ivy slammed her helmet into the dugout.

I went back up to bat. Two outs now. The big pitcher windmilled and threw a hard one. *CRACK!* I smashed it and chugged for two bases. A double!

I was in scoring position, with the best hitter in New England up. But that chicken Beefsteak signaled his catcher to intentionally walk Bridget. Ivy and Erin *buk-buk*-ed and flapped their arms in the dugout. Mrs. Loomer made them stop.

Blair came up to bat. "Come on, Blair," I shouted. "Help yourself out!"

Hambone threw a hard one. It curved in—*SLAP!* The ball smashed Blair on the back.

Mr. Reed was on the plate umpire in a flash. "That was deliberate!" he screamed.

Blair sat in the dirt, huffing to catch her breath. Mrs. Loomer tried to stick an icebag on her ribs but Blair shook her off.

Beefsteak blasted out of his dugout like an erupting volcano. The umpire lectured him and Mr. Reed, then resumed the game.

Hambone's face was wet. I couldn't tell if it was from sweat or tears.

Blair took first, Bridget moved to second. We had bases loaded, two outs.

The big pitcher struck Leigha out on three pitches. So much for Hambone's control problem.

After the first inning, the score was 0–0. But the Terminators had done their damage—Ivy was in a foul mood and Blair had a bruise the size of a melon on her back.

Chapter NINETEEN

Nikki's parents arrived with Tori's dad in the third inning.

"Can Nikki and Tori play now?" I asked Ginny.

"No," she said. "That jerk wouldn't let us even list them as subs."

"Do you think the others will get here in time?" I said. We were still waiting for Erin's dad to arrive from Boston, and Jenna's mom, who was meandering down from New Hampshire.

Ginny's face was dark with anger. "They'd better. I didn't work this hard to put this team together, only to have some two-bit loser beat us on a technicality."

"Oh," I said.

"MadCat, forget what I said, okay? It's not your problem."

I hugged her. "But you're a thousand percent right."

She hugged me back. "I know."

• • • • •

Blair held the Terminators hitless through six innings. We started the seventh inning, tied at 0–0.

Blair struck out the first batter. Julie got the second out on a pop fly to deep second base. Then Hambone came up. She swung her bat like a caveman's club.

Blair pitched a sizzler. Hambone swung and *CRACK!*

SLAP! Blair took the line drive on the knee. She went down. I went for the ball. Too late—Hambone made first base.

I bellowed, "Time!" and ran to the pitcher's circle. Half the dugout ran with me. My mother pushed through the kids to get to Blair.

Blair's face was frozen—her teeth clenched, her eyes wide, her skin pasty. My mother carefully felt around her knee.

"It hit her above the knee," Mr. Reed said. "It's just a bruise."

"She needs ice," my mother said. As a nurse, she knew all about these things. "You don't want swelling in the deep muscle."

"When the inning is over," Mr. Reed said.

"She's got to come out of the game now," Mom said. "Look at the size of that." *That* was a lump the size of—well, a softball.

"She can't come out of the game," Ginny whispered. "Rules let us play with eight. But if we drop to seven, we have to forfeit."

"We can ice it when the inning is over." Mr. Reed helped Blair up. "Right, Blair?"

Blair hobbled toward the pitcher's plate, barely able to walk. "Sure," she said.

My mother grabbed Ginny's arm. "Talk some sense into him."

Ginny just smiled. "Thanks, Anita. Why don't you go back to your seat?"

My mother's mouth opened, as if she was about to argue. "Mom, go on back," I whispered.

She shook her head as she walked to the sidelines.

"Jess, warm up," Ginny said.

"Blair can pitch," Mr. Reed said.

I was the only kid close enough to hear what Ginny said to Mr. Reed. "Let's not be *too* ridiculous, Jim."

He stared at her for a minute. Then he said, "Blair, go to first. Bridget to second, Julie to left center."

Blair hobbled to first while I warmed up Jess. Blair looked a little better. But Jess looked like she was going to throw up. She pulled a couple of pills out of her pocket.

"What're those?" I asked. They smelled like grape candy.

"Just some baby ibuprofen," she said. "Headache stuff."

● ● ● ● ●

Jess walked the batter in four straight pitches. I was eating dirt to keep the ball from going to the backstop.

I didn't recognize the next batter—she was new to the

Terminators this year. I walked the ball out to Jess. "You struck that girl out four times last year," I said.

"I did?" Jess squinted at the batter. "I don't remember her."

"Yeah," I lied. "Twice in Townsend, once in Pepperell, and once in Ashby. Don't you remember? She twisted like a knot, going after your changeup."

Jess looked at the batter again. "Oh, yeah," she said, grinning.

On the first pitch, the runners took off. I whipped the ball to Kayleigh, aiming for the inside of the bag. But there was daylight between Kayleigh's glove and the ground. The ball bounced under her glove, then out to left field.

Hambone didn't bother to slide into third—she tagged and dug for home. Julie whipped the ball to me from short left field. I went down for the tag.

Hambone slid high and late, hitting me like a bulldozer. I spun through a whirlwind of stars and dust, and flipped over home plate.

The umpire stuck his face down, so close I could smell coffee breath. "Show me, Catch."

I held out my glove.

"OUT!" he bellowed.

"You okay, MadCat?" It was Ivy, yanking my mask off, wiping my face.

"Fine," I said, even though I felt like I had been rototilled. I waved at the fans, then saw another wonderful sight.

Jenna's mother was behind home plate, opening her purse so she could show the Tournament Director her driver's license.

•   •   •   •   •

"You sure you're okay?" Mom asked. She felt my shoulders, my neck, my arms.

I yanked away. "I'm fine. Jeepers, Mom."

"That tackle at home plate was uncalled for. Unsportsmanlike."

"That wasn't a tackle. It was a bad slide," I said. "She just tried to get to the plate. And I wouldn't let her."

"Someone ought to say something," Mom said. "If your coaches won't, I will."

"NO!" I yelped.

"Why not?" Mom said.

"Because—" I looked my mother in the eye. I hadn't noticed until that moment that I had gotten as tall as her. "Because *that* is how you play to win."

Then I joined my team in the dugout.

Chapter TWENTY

Bottom of the seventh, score still at 0–0. Kayleigh grabbed Bridget's bat and headed out to hit.

"It's too heavy," Mrs. Loomer nagged at her.

"It's lucky," Kayleigh said. "Everything Bridget touches is lucky."

The girls on the bench started rubbing their hats and gloves and bats all over Bridget. She just grinned and took it.

Hambone almost hit Kayleigh with the first pitch. The second pitch came down the middle. *CRACK!* Kayleigh slammed it to deep short. The shortstop fielded it and threw but Kayleigh was down the line like a greyhound.

"Safe!" the base umpire yelled.

We took an automatic out for the ninth batter we didn't have.

One out, one on. Ivy came up. Kayleigh took off for second and slid in safely.

Ivy bunted the next pitch down the first baseline. Hambone tagged Ivy out but Kayleigh made it to third.

Two outs. Jess came up. She hadn't had a hit all weekend.

"Murder-ize it!" Ivy yelled.

"Slammer-ize it!" Julie shouted.

"Killer-ize it!" Leigha hollered.

"Come on, Jess," I yelled. "*Termin*-ize it!"

Hambone pitched. Jess swung and *SMACK!* The ball flew. Soaring into the setting sun, rising into the air—all the way over the left field fence!

I screamed so hard, I almost turned my lungs inside out. HOME RUN!

Kayleigh scored the game-winning run—we only needed one. But we waited for Jess to circle the bases, then jump on home plate. Then we screamed for a minute straight.

It was seven-thirty when we left the dugout. The Commissioner had extended the deadline for verifying our roster until nine o'clock.

We sat in the grass to wait for Erin's father, who was working his way north through what the radio was calling "one of the biggest traffic jams in Boston history."

● ● ● ● ●

"How did you do it?" I asked Jess. Even Bridget hadn't hit one clear over the fence yet.

Jess flexed her arm, popping up a bicep the size of a plum tomato. "I've been lifting weights," she said. She ate two more of those purple pills.

"Still got a headache?" I asked.

"It's almost gone," she said.

We sat in a circle, eating pizza, swatting mosquitoes, and waiting for Erin's dad. The Terminators sat across the field, swatting their own mosquitoes.

"He'll only make it if he has a helicopter," Mom had said to Bump on the phone. "A tanker truck overturned—all the major routes going north are blocked."

Ginny and Mr. Reed were practically on their knees, begging the Commissioner to extend the time. But she said she had to report the winner of the National Qualifier to Kentucky by nine o'clock.

I lay back in the grass and dozed. Next thing I knew, Julie was shaking me awake. "It's time for our execution," she said.

The fields were dark, except for the one we had played on. All the other age divisions had received their trophies and their berths to Nationals, and gone home.

Erin was crying. "It's my fault if we don't go to Kentucky."

"No, it is not," Mr. Reed said. His voice sounded like cold steel. "It's that bush-league blowhard's fault. If we don't get our berth, I'm going to—"

"Dad," Blair said. "Don't. Please."

A car beeped as it pulled into the parking lot nearest our field.

A tall man with white hair and glasses got out. He wore sweatpants and a ratty T-shirt. He looked familiar but I couldn't place him.

The passenger side door opened and another man got out—a man I knew better than my own heart. "Bump!" I yelled.

I started running and everyone followed me. I hugged my father so hard, he had to sit back down in the car.

"Mr. Tzachuk?" Jess said. "What are you doing here?"

Mr. Tzachuk was the principal of Nissitissit Middle School. I didn't recognize him in goof-off clothes. "Mr. Campione called to tell me there was a problem with our report cards," he said.

Ginny Page introduced Mr. Tzachuk to the Director and Conference Commissioner. She passed over Coach Beefsteak like he was a piece of manure.

Mr. Tzachuk handed the Commissioner a piece of paper. "This is a notarized affidavit," he said. "It's from the town clerk of Norwich, affirming that Nissitissit Middle School is indeed in Norwich, New Hampshire."

He handed her another letter. "This affirms that Jessica Page, Erin Quin, Victoria Connor, Nikki Norhanian, Madelyn Catherine Campione, and Jenna Leah Pappas are all students of Nissitissit Middle School. I trust that satisfies your residency requirement."

"You bet," she said. "I'll fax these along with the roster to the National Office."

Beefsteak said a word that I'll never repeat, then disappeared into the darkness.

Every girl on the team insisted on hugging Bump. They wanted him to watch us get our trophies but the field was in the middle of the complex. Too far for my father to drag his bad leg. "I'll watch from here," he said.

"Please," Blair begged. "I'll push your wheelchair."

"Don't," I whispered, pulling her away from Bump. "You're embarrassing him."

The Director pulled up on a golf cart. "Hop in, Mr. Campione. You rode all the way from Norwich. We're not about to leave you in the parking lot."

I held my breath for what seemed like forever. Then Bump said, "Thanks. I'd like that."

Accepting the trophy for winning the twelve-and-under NFS National Qualifier was the proudest moment of my life. And the happiest, because my mother and my father were there.

And my team, all of whom— even Ivy—were my best friends in the whole world.

Chapter TWENTY-ONE

The Tuesday morning after our big win, Mom made us an awesome omelet—eggs and cheese wrapped around garden asparagus that she said she had to "wade through a jungle to find."

"The lower forty needs weeding," Mom said to Bump.

"Let it go," he mumbled, then rolled over in his recliner.

I cleaned up the breakfast dishes, polished my trophy for the fourteenth time, then called Jess. Rick said she had an appointment with the bone doctor.

"You mean an orthopedist?" Because of Bump being sick and Mom being a nurse, I not only knew the word, I could spell it if I had to.

"Whatever."

"Why? Did she break something?"

Rick paused, then said, "Just a checkup, I think."

I went out to the backyard and stared at the garden. It was a mess of crabgrass and weeds. Somewhere in the tangle were the neat rows of plants and seeds that Blair and I had planted weeks ago.

"Let it go," Bump had said.

Let it go, I thought. My legs still ached from catching all weekend and my ribs screamed from where Hambone had bulldozed me. It would be nice to just sit and vegetate in front of the television for once. But letting the garden go would be like letting Bump go.

I sprayed my oldest Sting cap with bug repellent, grabbed a water bottle and my CD player, then waded into the jungle that used to be our garden.

● ● ● ● ●

When Blair showed up an hour later, I had only managed to weed one row of tomatoes. That left me beets, squash, beans, pumpkins, corn, peppers, eggplant, cabbage, broccoli, brussels sprouts, and radishes. And asparagus, onions, carrots, and who knows what else—Blair had planted every seed she could find so I wasn't sure what was growing in there.

"Look at this mess!" I sighed.

"I'll help!" Blair promptly yanked out a bean plant.

"That's not a weed!" I yelled.

"Sorry." She tried to replant it but only managed to break the stalk.

Just as I was about to scream, Mugger showed up. "Hi," she said. She looked at Blair sideways.

"This is Mugger," I said. "Her real name is Amanda. Mugger, this is Blair Reed."

"I know," Mugger said. "I saw her picture in the newspaper yesterday."

"Oh," I said.

Blair just bit her lip and smiled.

"Mugger used to play—"

"I know," Blair said. "Sorry."

I demolished a clump of crabgrass. I couldn't bear the look on Mugger's face.

"So I guess you don't want to pitch, MadCat," Mugger said.

"You're a pitcher, MadCat?" Blair said.

I yanked another weed. My mind was like the garden—too many things going on in there, choking me. "I'm just fooling around with it," I said. "Mugger's learning how, and I'm kind of doing it with her."

Blair smiled at Mugger. "That's cool. Good for you." She grabbed the trowel from me. "I'll weed. You go help Mugger."

"Blair, you don't know how to tell the weeds from the plants," I said.

"I'll figure it out," she said.

"How?"

Blair smiled and pointed to the patio. Bump was sitting in a lounge chair, staring up at the sky. I hadn't seen him come out. "Your father can tell me," she said. "Come on, go pitch."

So we pitched and Blair weeded. Bump watched us, every once in a while identifying weeds for Blair. When Blair got tired of weeding, she caught for Mugger while I weeded. Then Mugger weeded while Blair caught for me.

Me pitching to Blair Reed was like me modeling a bikini in front of a movie star—a sick joke.

"You're doing great, MadCat," Blair said.

"Oh yeah, compared to the turnips out there, I'm a real star," I said. "But compared to you—"

"Don't!" Blair said. "I hate it when people do that to me."

"Do what to you?" I asked.

"Nothing. Excuse me." Blair kicked off her muddy shoes, and disappeared into our house.

I sat at the edge of Bump's chair and stole a sip of his iced tea. "Is she weird or what?" I whispered. "I didn't do anything to her."

"You compared yourself to her," Bump said.

"So what's wrong with that?" I asked. "She should love it. She always comes out on top."

"Which is why she hates it," Bump said.

● ● ● ● ●

By Friday morning, we had gotten the garden down to bare ground and rows of vegetable plants.

Blair was disappointed. "Why is the lettuce dead but the other vegetables aren't even ripe yet?" she asked.

"Most things, like tomatoes and squash, appear late in July or early August. Lettuce, peas, even spinach like cooler temperatures, which is why we had them in June," I explained. "We'll plant a second crop at the end of August, and have them again in October. If it doesn't snow early," I added.

Blair groaned. Mugger laughed. Mugger laughed at Blair a lot. I didn't get it—Blair never seemed a barrel of *chuckles* to me. But if she tweaked Mugger's funny bone, who was I to try to figure it out?

Every morning after weeding, Blair gave Mugger and me pitching workouts. A total waste of time for me, but Blair and Mugger seemed to like it so I pretended to.

Even Bump seemed to enjoy it, coming out to the patio to watch. Except on Thursday, when he watched from inside the family room because his leg was totally shut down. When I found a brochure for battery-operated wheelchairs near his recliner, I asked Bump if he was getting one.

"I'm not in the grave yet," he snapped.

"Don't talk like that," I said. "That's mean."

"Life is mean," Bump said. But an hour later, he made me strawberry shortcake with real whipped cream. He never did answer me about the wheelchair.

Mugger had a game Friday night. Blair decided we should go cheer her on.

"No!" Mugger said.

"Why not?" Blair said.

Mugger just shrugged.

"We'll make her nervous," I said. The whole idea made me nervous—taking the best pitcher I had ever seen to a rec game? Blair would probably turn herself inside out, laughing.

"Why would we make you nervous?" Blair asked. "We're friends, right?"

Mugger shrugged, then said, "I guess."

"Okay, it's settled, then," Blair said. While I raked the last of the weeds into a pile, Blair tried to teach Mugger how to do a changeup.

Wait until Blair sees rec ball, where all *the pitches are changeups,* I thought. *Will she still want to be Mugger's friend, then?*

Chapter TWENTY-TWO

Mugger's team was called the Hurricanes. They wore sky-blue shirts that didn't match their stormy name but no one seemed to care.

During warm-ups, the throwing was wild, the catching was spotty, and the fielding seemed to be a matter of luck. But Mellissa was patient with each player, showing one how to hold her glove, another how to get her backside down for a ground ball.

They weren't a tournament team, that was for sure. But they had a good time, chasing balls and cheering each other on. "Not what you're used to, are they, MadCat?" Mellissa said.

"No. But it's supposed to be just for fun," I added quickly.

"You have more fun when you learn something," Mellissa said. "And these kids are learning."

"Cool," I said, too cheerfully.

"You been working on your pitching?" Mellissa asked.

"Mugger makes me," I said.

Mellissa laughed. "Yeah, Mugger. She'll surprise you tonight, I think."

She had surprised me all week. Mugger—the girl who barely talked—had somehow become good friends with Blair—the girl who had the personality of iceberg lettuce. Blair was with Mugger at the bench now, tightening Mugger's glove and giving her a pep talk.

"Why does Blair like Mugger so much?" I had asked Bump that morning.

"Mugger doesn't expect anything from her," he said.

"Neither do I," I said.

"You don't?" Bump said. "Think about it, Cat."

I didn't expect anything from Blair Reed—except for her to *be* Blair Reed—the best pitcher in New England, and maybe beyond. I guessed that was a lot to expect from a twelve-year-old kid.

I held my breath as Mugger went to the pitcher's circle and got ready to throw the first pitch. I wasn't sure what her new team expected from her.

I just hoped she could show them something good.

● ● ● ● ●

Mugger struck out the first six batters she faced.

"Holy cannoli," I said to Mellissa. "She's better than me!"

"Yes and no," Mellissa said. "She's got a lot better control. But you're a whole lot stronger. She's got to work on throwing hard."

"Throwing hard! She's striking everyone out!"

Mellissa smiled. "MadCat, they don't see windmill pitching in rec ball. What would happen if she pitched in a tournament game?"

"She'd get creamed," I finally said.

"Yep," Mellissa said. "Today. But soon enough, both you and she will be pitching at tournament level."

"Forget that. Even if I could possibly—in a million billion years—get good enough, the Sting does't need me to pitch. Not with Blair here."

"Does that bother you?" Mellissa asked.

"Not anymore," I said. "We are going to Nationals, after all."

Mellissa laughed. "If the Hurricanes win the rec league, we might get to go to Concord to play in the Friendship Tournament."

"Does that bother you?" I asked.

"Nope," Mellissa said. "Good kids, all the bubble gum I can chew, and all the cheering my eardrums can take—hey, I wouldn't trade it for the world."

Liar, I thought, though I would never say it. Mellissa Kubit loved to win as much as anyone. And so did

Mugger, even though she kept quiet about it.

Ivy had said that *being fair but not winning kind of stinks.* But, when you came down to it, whether it be tournament ball, the Nationals, or Mugger's game going on right in front of me—losing does stink.

Even if no one would admit it.

•　•　•　•　•

Mugger's team won the game, 20–3. Mugger slammed the ball every time she got up. She struck out ten, walked eight, and gave up six hits. Sam Murphy cheered loudly from the sidelines. When I waved hi at him, he turned his back on me.

After the game, Mugger had to help her team load equipment in Mellissa's truck. Blair and I were tossing a ball back and forth when I spotted a familiar figure beyond the center field fence. "Hey, Mac!" I ran to meet him. He was walking his dog, a pug named Daisy.

"What are you doing here, MadCat?" he asked.

"I came to watch Mugger," I said. My heart felt funny, like I had run too fast without realizing it.

"Yeah. I saw a couple innings," Mac said. "I didn't know she could pitch. She looked halfway decent."

I scratched Daisy's jowls. She growled happily in the back of her throat. "Well, I just wanted to say hi," I said. I started back toward Blair. She was tossing the ball to herself, pretending not to notice Mac.

"MadCat! Wait," Coach said. "I'd give anything to tell

Amanda—Mugger—how proud I am of her. But her father would wring my neck. So, could you tell her for me?"

"Sure," I said.

Mac jiggled Daisy's leash, and she followed him off.

"Mac!" I called out.

He turned and looked at me.

"I wish you hadn't quit the team," I said.

"Is that what they told you girls? That I *quit*?"

"Yeah," I said. "At least I thought—" But now I didn't know what to think. "Anyway, I'm sorry you don't coach the Sting anymore," I said.

"I am, too," he said. Then he and Daisy walked away.

STING TRAVELS TO KENTUCKY

The Northeast Sting travels to Louisville, Kentucky, this week to participate in the National Fastpitch Softball World Series.

"Playing in a national tournament is a thrill and a challenge that our girls will remember for the rest of their lives," said Sting coach Jim Reed. "The team has worked hard to prove that players from cold-weather states can compete with the best . . .

Chapter TWENTY-THREE

I was so hot, I was sweating like a hog at a pig roast.

"Ladies don't sweat," Mom would say. "They glow."

"Focus, MadCat," Mac would say. But Mac wasn't in Kentucky with us.

"It is so hot!" I said.

"It's awesome!" Blair said. "I haven't been warm since we moved to New Hampshire. Maybe I'll finally thaw out."

"It stinks!" said Jenna. "Look at Nikki's pits. She's pouring sweat."

"You're the one who stinks, eating those jalapeños," Nikki grumbled. "You burp one more time and you'll blow us back to New Hampshire."

"Blame MadCat," Jenna said. "She told me I needed the vitamins. We are playing in Nationals, you know."

Nationals. Even in Louisville's 95-degree heat, the word made me shiver.

We waited in front of the airport for Mr. Reed and Mrs. Loomer to pick us up in the rental vans. Some parents had flown down with us, but most were driving down to save money.

"Our crummy car can barely make the drive to Norwich for practice," Ivy had told me. "My mother can't drive to Kentucky."

Mom decided to drive Bump's van instead of flying. That way Ms. O'Riley could make the trip. "Come with us, Phil. We've got plenty of room," Mom said.

"I feel like crap, Anita," he said.

"So you might as well feel like crap in Kentucky," Mom snapped.

"So I can sit around in a hotel room for six days?" Bump complained. "Staring at four walls? I can do that here."

"You won't have to stay in the hotel," I said. "Mr. Reed said the complexes are handi—" I coughed to erase the word *handicapped*. Bump hated it. "The complexes are really easy to get to."

In the end, it was Ivy who decided it. "You think I like being stuck in right field all the time? Sometimes you've got to swallow your pride, Mr. C. For the sake of the team."

Bump ignored her but I was about to beat the snot out of Ivy. Not that a smack from me would stop her.

"Or for the sake of your kid," Ivy continued. "You came

all the way to Lowell with us, you spineless cucumber. So come to Kentucky."

"Maybe," he said.

We left it at *maybe* for a couple of weeks. But when we packed the van, the wheelchair, walker, and cane went in with the luggage and coolers.

The team, coaches, and a couple of parents flew out on Sunday morning. The driving parents left at the same time. Everyone would be settled by Monday night, just in time for Opening Ceremonies.

Tuesday we would play our first game. I remembered how I had imagined it way back in April, the day after try-outs. The California girls squealing, the Texas girls sweating, the Arizona girls cursing. The Sting of little Norwich, New Hampshire stomping them all.

Except now when I saw myself squatting behind the plate, it was Blair Reed whipping in the fastballs—not Jessica Page.

● ● ● ● ●

A half hour after checking into the hotel, Mr. Reed drove us to a practice field.

"We just got here!" Julie moaned. "Can't we hang out here?"

"We came to play," Mr. Reed barked. "Not hang out."

For the past two weeks, Mr. Reed had been practicing us at noontime to get us used to playing in high heat. But New

Hampshire didn't know the meaning of high heat, not compared to Kentucky. It was mid-afternoon, under a baking sun. Mrs. Loomer made us all slather up with sunscreen. I felt like a piece of haddock, oiled up and stuck under the broiler.

Mrs. Loomer was knocking grounders at some of us while the rest chased fly balls with Mr. Reed.

"Where's the Crown Princess?" Ivy asked.

"Jess has an appointment," Mrs. Loomer said.

"What kind?" I asked. Jess hadn't said anything about an appointment on the flight down.

"Something personal. Now get to work." Mrs. Loomer blasted a ball right at me. I fielded it, then whipped it back in.

"Anybody know anything about an appointment?" I asked, when I got in line.

"Maybe she's getting highlights in her hair," Kayleigh said. "In case she gets on national television."

"If you get on national television, you'll break the camera," Jenna said. "Jeepers, Kay, you've still got lunch all over your face."

Kayleigh spit on her fingers and tried to wipe off the mustard she had been wearing since we flew over Pittsburgh.

Mrs. Loomer blasted a hard grounder to Leigha's left. She dove ten feet and snagged a ball that I would have needed a pole to stop.

Mrs. Loomer nailed one to my right side. I dove, like Leigha had. But all I came up with was a mouthful of dirt.

"Hey, Crabgrass. So what is Jess's problem?" Ivy whispered as she yanked me up.

"No problem," I said. But how could I know that for sure, now that Jess was keeping secrets from me, too?

•   •   •   •   •

Three hours later, we returned to the hotel. Mr. Reed refused to let us swim. "You're not using up all your energy in that blasted pool," he said. He ordered us to sit in the shade while we had an early supper. Afterwards, we would talk strategy.

I grabbed a sandwich and two oranges, and went to my room. Jess was lying on the bed, an ice pack on her shoulder. Her suitcase lay open in the corner, with seven brand-new pairs of athletic socks right on top. When I opened my suitcase, it stunk from the socks I had worn all through the Qualifier. I would wear them until we lost, and then I would wash them out, and wear them again until we lost.

I guess I was the only one playing this game now. But maybe Jess was right—maybe we were too good now for such dumb games, now that we were at Nationals.

I tossed Jess one of my oranges. "Where've you been? Kayleigh told everyone you were getting the fungus shaved off your toenails. But I said you were getting your facial hair plucked."

Jess laughed and tossed a pillow at me. "You scum. Hey, want to hear a secret?"

"Only if it's good." I flopped down and peeled my orange.

"Mom got me a session with Denise LeMansard," she said.

"Who the heck is Denise Le-whatever?" The orange tasted sweet beyond belief.

"She's practically the most famous pitching coach in the United States," Jess said.

"So how'd you get hooked up with Ms. Pitching U.S.A.?"

"My mother read she was going to be here, scouting the high school girls. So Mom hired her to give me a pitching lesson," Jess said.

"Jeepers, that must have cost a lot of money," I said.

"It comes from my college fund. My mom says it's an investment in my future." Jess squealed, and jumped off the bed.

"What!" I yelped. "Don't tell me we have cockroaches!"

"No, the stupid bag of ice broke. We'll make Ivy sleep on that bed tonight." Jess's throwing arm was deep red from the ice. There was a Band-Aid on the tip of her shoulder.

"What's that?" I said.

"Duh, MadCat," Jess said, making a baby voice. "Haven't you ever had a boo-boo?"

I looked her in the eye. "What kind of boo-boo is it, Jess?"

She looked away. "Just a scratch," she said. Then she went into the bathroom and shut the door.

Chapter TWENTY-FOUR

The parents who drove to Kentucky had arrived in the middle of the night. When I went to my parents' room the next morning, Bump was still asleep.

Mom gave me a big bowl of homemade granola, topped with bananas and Kentucky-fresh blueberries. I told her about Jess's bag of ice and the Band-Aid. "Something's wrong," I said.

"That's what I've been thinking," Mom said. "But Ginny says it's just a little tendonitis, and it's under control."

"So I should stop worrying?" I said.

"You shouldn't even start worrying," Mom said. "That's our job, not yours."

"Who's worrying?" a groggy voice said.

"Bump!"

He needed a shave, his hair stuck out on the back of his

head, and his left eye was crusty. But my father looked better than anything, even the Kentucky-fresh blueberries.

"You coming to the game?" I asked, after I hugged him for a minute straight.

"Cat, your mom and Joan O'Riley had a thousand miles to browbeat me into it," he said, laughing. "Bring it on!"

"Bring it on!" I echoed, suddenly without a worry in my head. I wasn't even worried about losing.

I just wanted to play.

• • • • •

Game day was hotter than Jenna's jalapeños.

"Who needs to warm up?" Julie moaned. "Stick a fork in me. I'm way overdone."

"Shut up with your whining," Ivy said. "Think about being me, for once."

"What, being psycho?" Jenna laughed.

"Being a catcher," Ivy said.

Mr. Reed had told her to pull on the equipment so she could warm up Blair. "Sorry, MadCat," Ivy had said, then raced to get dressed.

Sorry, Ivy, I thought. Mr. Reed had already told me to throw and hit a few balls, then sit in the shade with my parents. He wanted me out of the heat until game time because I would be catching.

The complex where the 12U teams were playing was amazing. There were eight softball fields with closed-in dugouts, red-clay infields, and something you don't often see in New England—real outfield fences. The concession stands sold everything from sweatpants to sunscreen to bagels with cream cheese. The bathrooms had flush toilets and hot and cold water.

Everywhere you went, you could hear balls slapping leather, bats whacking balls, and girls cheering—the sweet sounds of summer softball.

The only thing this complex didn't have was shade. The nearest trees were a block away, in the playground. My parents went out to buy a portable shade tent. Meanwhile, Jenna's mom helped me find a cool patch behind a small length of stockade fencing.

I was trying to rest when I heard familiar voices on the other side of the fence.

Ginny Page called Mr. Reed the ugliest name I had ever heard! I hadn't realized that Ginny even knew words like that, let alone allowed them out of her mouth.

Mr. Reed didn't say anything but I could hear him breathing—slow and long, like I sound when I'm trying not to throw up. "You through?" he finally said.

"No, I'm not through! We had an understanding," Ginny said. "Jessica is to get equal exposure."

"You fool! I'm doing Jess a favor. This team will pound her. Tomorrow she'll show better."

"I've got people here today," Ginny said. "They want to see her pitch. Now."

"Damn it," Mr. Reed said. "You promised we'd coordinate this."

"It came up suddenly," Ginny said. "You can't blame me

for taking advantage. That's what you taught me, isn't it?"

They walked off, still arguing.

When I returned to the field, Ginny grabbed me. "Get your stuff on," she said. "You need to warm up Jess."

"Mr. Reed said Blair was—"

"Mr. Reed was wrong," Ginny snapped. "Move it, MadCat. She's only got twenty minutes."

She didn't even have that, it turned out. Five minutes before game time, we had to line up at the third baseline, across from the Orange County Heat. Because it was our first game, we were being introduced to the fans.

Jess hadn't even started full motion yet. "Are you gonna be ready?" I whispered.

"Do I have a choice?" Jess said. "Mr. Reed really loused this one up." Jess chewed a couple of those purple pills.

"Headache again?" I whispered.

"Yeah. From the stupid heat." She popped in a fat white tablet.

"What's that for?" I asked. "Your shoulder?"

Her eyes popped, like I had pinched her. "Who said anything about my shoulder? There's nothing wrong with my arm."

"So what's that big pill for, then?" I asked.

"The headache pills make my stomach acidy," she said. "No big deal."

I hoped not.

• • • • •

When Ivy saw the lineup, she repeated some of Ginny's nastiest phrases.

"I'm sorry," I said.

"Shut up, MadCat," Ivy said. "You think I'd apologize if you were stuck out in right field and I got to catch?"

Over the first few innings, Jess pitched well. But the Orange County Heat nickel-and-dimed their way onto base with a walk here, a slash there, a base-hit bunt here and there.

The temperature pushed one hundred. I felt like steamed broccoli under my equipment. Mom poured drinks and doused us with cold cloths in the dugout.

We went into the bottom of the last inning without a hit. The Heat had picked their way to a two-run lead.

The first two outs came before I even got my equipment off. Julie flied out to deep short while Jenna struck out. The pitcher was hotter than heatstroke—she was working on a perfect game. We hadn't had a base runner yet.

"Slammer-ize it," I yelled at Ivy as she grabbed her bat.

"Yeah, right," she said.

"Hey! You giving up?" Kayleigh asked.

Ivy whipped around so fast, she made the first breeze I had felt all day.

"You talking to me?" Ivy said, getting in Kayleigh's face.

Kayleigh backed away. "I think so," she whispered.

"Okay, then," Ivy said. "I'll slammer-ize it."

Ivy singled to right field, ruining Heatstroke's no-hitter.

Jess went up to bat, holding her stomach. She was nervous

about ending the game, I knew. Meanwhile, I stood in the on-deck circle, half-hoping Jess would make the last out so I wouldn't have to.

"Hey, Cat!" Bump stood at the fence—no wheelchair, walker, or cane. It must have taken him three innings to make it all the way from the shade tent beyond center field, using the fence to hold himself up.

"What are you doing here?" I asked.

"I came to see you knock in some runs," he said.

"You wasted your time," I said. "Miss Heatstroke has struck me out twice."

"Hey, I didn't ride a thousand miles to see some pea pod from California tie my kid into knots. Go show these surfers how we play ball in the Granite State."

Jess drew a walk. My turn to grab my stomach.

"Slammer-ize it!" Bump yelled.

I got in my batter's stance and stared down at Heatstroke. Both times I had struck out on inside pitches. She'd be likely to go there again.

I crowded the plate, daring her to choke me. As Heatstroke began her windup, she grinned.

Gotcha, she was thinking.

Gotcha back, I hoped.

As her arm came down, I opened my stance by stepping my front foot toward third base. The pitch came in, heading for the inside corner.

I slammed it down the third base line.

The Sting fans went nuts! Ivy scored easily. Mr. Page

held me at first until he saw the throw going into the plate. I took second base standing, my eye on home plate where Jess was sliding in under the tag.

Safe! Game tied!

Jess grabbed her stomach, then spit something up. The umpire said something to her but Jess waved him off.

"You okay?" I yelled. She gave me the thumbs-up.

Bridget blasted the ball but the center fielder caught it at the fence. Tie score, extra innings.

As I came in for my catcher's equipment, Bump was still at the fence. He clung to the chain link and did a one-legged jig.

The heck with the score—I felt like I just won the game.

Chapter TWENTY-FIVE

The game was now in International Tiebreaker.

"What the heck is that?" Ivy asked.

"It's to keep the games moving along," Blair said. "If you're tied at the end of regulation play, then the team at bat automatically puts a runner on second base. If we go into the next inning still tied, the runner starts at third base. This goes on until the tie finally breaks."

Ginny, Mr. Reed, and my mother were in a three-way discussion. They thought they were whispering but, as I put on my equipment, I caught every word.

Mom wanted me taken out at catcher before I got heatstroke. Mr. Reed wanted to put Blair in to pitch and save the game. Ginny insisted that Jess be allowed to keep pitching because it was hers to win or lose.

Finally Mr. Reed asked Mom and Ginny to leave the dugout. He saw me staring at him, my mouth open. "I'm sorry, MadCat," he said. "Your mother's been a huge help but—"

"It's okay," I said. Coaching stunk—you couldn't make everyone happy at the same time, so most of the time, no one was happy.

I walked the game ball out to Jess. "You okay?" I asked.

"Look over there," she said, nodding to first base side. "See the guy with the big belly? He's from the University of Iowa. And the woman in the pink shorts, she's from UCLA. Here to see me," Jess said. She dug into her pocket and took out a couple of those grape-pills. "Pretty cool, huh?"

"Cool," I said. "Didn't you just take a couple of those?"

"They're only baby-pills. You need to take a lot to make the pain stop," Jess said. "Come on, let's show everyone what New Hampshire is made of."

I walked back to home plate, wondering exactly what New Hampshire *was* made of. Snow, mountains, sun? Hearty vegetables and hearty people?

Or headaches and purple baby-pills?

●　●　●　●　●

We held strong for three more innings. Orange County replaced Heatstroke with a pitcher who smiled all the time so I called her Sunstroke.

Ginny must have won the argument because Jess stayed

in the game. She pitched harder and better than I had ever seen her. Whatever list college people put twelve-year-olds on was sure to include Jessica Page of Norwich, New Hampshire.

In the top of the eleventh inning, Jess gave up a measly single. With the tiebreaker runner on third, it was enough to score one run.

We went into the bottom of the inning, down 3–2. Jess had been the last batter of the tenth, so she went to third base to be the tiebreaker.

"Knock me in, MadCat," she pleaded.

Even with Bump at the fence to cheer me on, I struck out. One out, one on.

"Knock me in, Bridget," Jess pleaded.

The Heat intentionally walked Bridget. Even though she hadn't hit in this game, somehow word had filtered all the way to California about her mighty bat. One out, two on.

"Knock me in, Blair," Jess pleaded.

Blair tried to bunt Jess in. It was almost too perfect a bunt, whirling in the clay on the first baseline. Sunstroke was on it in a flash, tagging Blair out, then looking Jess back to third base. Two outs, two on.

"Knock me in, Kayleigh," Jess pleaded. Kayleigh was batting sixth only because Leigha had gotten diarrhea from the heat and had to sub out. She had the lowest batting average on the team.

Mr. Reed called time. He called Kayleigh and Jess to

him but spent most of his time talking to Jess.

"Crap. I don't believe it." Ivy dug her nails into my arm.

"What?" I yelped.

"Shush," Blair said.

Ivy looked at Blair. "Your old man knows Kayleigh's not gonna hit. So he's telling Jess to steal home, right?"

Blair nodded.

I said a word that Mom would have killed me for—though she probably would have to agree. Stealing home in fastpitch softball is almost impossible. The diamond is small, the pitching is fast, and the girls are smart.

On the first pitch, Jess faked a lead, then slid back into third base. She cried out and grabbed her ankle. "Time!" Mr. Reed called. Jess limped around third base, flexing her foot.

"You want a sub?" Mrs. Loomer called.

"We don't have one left," Mr. Reed said, loudly enough for the whole field to hear. That was a lie. Erin hadn't gotten into the game yet.

Ball one on Kayleigh. The second pitch was strike one. As the pitcher walked the ball back to the circle, she glanced at Jess. Instead of taking a lead, Jess was rubbing her ankle and looking like she might cry.

The next pitch was ball two. Kayleigh almost swung but held back, just in time. The catcher glanced at Jess, then walked the ball to the pitcher.

Jess took off like a shot.

It was a race to the plate—Jess versus the catcher.

They got there at the same time, Jess sliding head first, the catcher diving on her belly, with her glove extended.

"OUT!" the umpire yelled.

Mr. Reed ripped his hat into pieces. Then he walked over to the fence, away from everyone.

Jess rolled over on her stomach and started throwing up. None of the kids would go near her because it was a private moment, even if it was right on home plate. And it was gross.

But Jessica Page was my best friend so I got to her before Ginny or my mother made it onto the field.

Jess was sheet-white.

Her puke was blood-red.

Chapter TWENTY-SIX

Jessica Page was dying.

I was sure of it. They had taken her by ambulance to the hospital, then rushed her to the Intensive Care Unit. My mother works in the ICU so I know that's where people go when they're so sick or injured, they might die at any moment.

The whole team and their families had tried to squeeze into the ICU waiting room. Finally Mrs. Loomer sent them all back to the hotel. "We're disturbing the other families here," she said.

It was decided that Bump and I would stay and wait because Mom had gone in with Ginny and Mr. Page to help them understand what the doctor was telling them.

And because I was Jess's best friend.

"Jess will be okay," my mother said an hour later, as she

pried me out of Bump's arms. I had fallen asleep, making a puddle of tears and clay on my father's shirt.

"You promise?" I said.

"Absolutely. They've decided she doesn't need to be transfused, so they're moving her to the pediatric unit."

"What happened, Anita?" Bump asked.

"Jess has one heck of a bleeding ulcer," Mom said. "She's had tendonitis in her shoulder for most of the season and has been taking anti-inflammatories—"

"You mean those purple pills?" I asked. "She said those were for her headaches."

"The doctor had already prescribed some pills. Apparently they weren't enough to handle the pain. So, on her own, Jess bought baby ibuprofen—those purple pills—and has been eating them like candy. On top of her prescribed medication."

"But that's all shoulder stuff. How did she get an ulcer?" I asked.

"Anti-inflammatories can be tough on your stomach," Mom said. "Jess was taking two or three times the correct dose without anyone knowing it. Ripped a hole in her stomach."

"Why didn't she tell anyone she was in so much pain?" I asked.

My mother looked at Bump. Her eyes were so sad, they broke my heart. "Because she was afraid she wouldn't be allowed to pitch," my mother finally said.

Then she started to cry.

• • • • •

Mr. Reed called a team meeting that night. "Jess is going to be okay," he said. "But let this be a lesson for everyone."

I raised my hand. "What kind of lesson?" I asked.

"That should be obvious," Mr. Reed said, giving me a look so cold it could put even Kentucky into a deep freeze.

But it wasn't obvious to me. *Don't keep secrets? Don't try to keep up with Blair Reed? Don't risk your life for a game?*

Mr. Reed reminded us that we had two games to play tomorrow, swore that Blair could pitch both with no problem, then ordered us to get a good night's sleep.

We arrived at the field the next morning, looking like we had been steamrollered. "You gonna be okay?" I asked Blair as I warmed her up.

"Sure. Why wouldn't I?" Blair answered.

"She wouldn't dare be anything but okay," Ivy said later. "Her father won't let her."

Blair was more than okay. She pitched a one-hit shutout in our first game, against the Breakers of New Mexico. Someone finally dared to pitch to Bridget and she rewarded them—and us—with a three-run homer.

We had a two-hour break, then came back to face a Florida team called the Devil Rays. Blair held them hitless but a costly error by Kayleigh allowed one run to score.

One run was all it took to beat us. Nationals were tough, we were all learning. Even Bridget couldn't collect a hit against the Devil Rays.

Nationals were about to get tougher. We had just finished the round-robin part of the tournament with one win and two losses. That put us in the middle part of the bracket for the championship round.

This round was double-elimination. That meant that two losses, then *BANG!* We would be back on the plane for New Hampshire.

● ● ● ● ●

When we returned to the hotel that afternoon, Jess was there. We boasted and laughed about beating the Breakers. No one said a word about losing to the Devil Rays.

Ginny bundled Jess in a blanket and let her sit on the patio with me. We munched on the melon slices Mom had sent along.

"So that boo-boo on your shoulder wasn't a scratch?" I asked.

"When we got off the plane, I couldn't lift my arm. It was frozen. No way would I ever be able to windmill," Jess said. "Mom was frantic—she had set up that session with Denise LeMansard. So we rushed to the emergency room and got me a cortisone shot. It worked, too. Didn't I pitch well?"

"You almost killed yourself! Doesn't that mean anything?"

"My father is ticked off about it," Jess said. "He and my mother had a huge fight. You know, the kind people get divorces from."

"Are you kidding me? Your parents are getting a divorce? Over softball?"

"Don't be dense, MadCat. Dad will cool off. But he's going home and taking my brothers and sister. He said they've all had enough."

"You probably should go, too," I said. "Go get better."

"No way. Mom and I are staying."

"To root the Sting on? Don't bother—we're not gonna last too long in the championship round."

"That—and other stuff," Jess said.

We heard splashing from the courtyard, then laughing. I looked down from the balcony. Kayleigh, Leigha, Ivy, and Erin were disobeying Mr. Reed's command that we stay out of the pool. They looked like they were having a great time.

"What other stuff?" I said, when I sat back down.

"Everyone's saying what a hustler I am, a real fighter. People have left messages, cards, college T-shirts. They're saying they want to keep in touch. Watch me develop."

"Cripes, Jess! You make it sound like blowing up your stomach was the best thing in the world!"

Jess pushed down the back of her lounge chair so she could lie flat. "I used to think that being Blair Reed was the best thing in the world," she said. "I threw my shoulder out all spring, all summer, trying to get better than her. And now look at me."

"I *am* looking at you," I said. "I just can't figure out what I'm seeing."

"The real winner," Jess said. "That's what you're seeing." She closed her eyes and drifted off to sleep.

I studied Jess as she slept. Same hair, same nose, same eyes that I always knew. Even the same skin, though she was a pasty pale under her tan.

But somehow, my best friend had disappeared.

Maybe Jess felt like a winner—but I felt like a loser.

Chapter TWENTY-SEVEN

The next two days were a whirl of clay dust, soggy humidity, and baking sun.

On Thursday, we lost our first game in the championship round, which put us into the losers' bracket. To get back to the winners' bracket and the top eight teams, we would have to win seven games in a row.

We played two more games that day. Blair pitched all of them, and I caught all but the last one. My mother and Ivy's mom cornered Mr. Reed and threatened to start driving home unless I got a break from the heat, and Ivy got a chance to catch.

No one said a word about Blair getting a break.

When we got back to the hotel that night, even Ivy was too tired to sneak into the pool. I told Jess how the games went, emphasizing all the good plays in the field and leaving out how incredibly Blair pitched.

Blair Reed was like a pitching machine. She never seemed tired or discouraged—she just pumped out strikes. She didn't smile much, but I figured she was conserving her energy.

Mr. Reed smiled all the time. Ivy said it was because now Her Majesty had the throne to herself.

For supper that night, Bump put together a scrumptious salad of arugula, romaine, and our garden tomatoes. Mom grilled some chicken breasts over Ms. O'Riley's camping stove. For dessert we had fresh peaches over frozen yogurt.

Ivy fell asleep with her face in the peaches.

On Friday, Blair pitched two games in the morning. Jess was well enough to sit under our shade tent and watch. Our wins put us halfway up the losers' bracket. We needed three more wins to make the semifinals.

Or one loss to go home.

We were scheduled to play at eight o'clock that night, under the lights. Mr. Reed wanted Blair back at the hotel to talk strategy. Somehow Mom nagged him into letting us take Blair for a couple of hours. "She needs a break from that man," she said to Bump.

Ms. O'Riley set up the camp stove so Bump could roast peppers, eggplant, and summer squash. He had marinated the vegetables—all from our garden—in olive oil and rosemary all day.

Bump moved between the grill and picnic table, his leg

shuffling—but not dragging. I poked my mother. "Where's the cane?" I whispered.

"I don't know," Mom whispered back. "Maybe that medication he got in Boston is actually working."

Maybe, I thought, hoped, and prayed.

Mom grilled extra-lean hamburgers, topped them with Jarlsberg cheese, and served them on crusty sourdough rolls.

"I'm moving in with you guys," Ivy said, slurping down her fifth chunk of pepper. "You know how to eat."

"Any time!" Bump said. He mussed Ivy's hair, then winked at Ms. O'Riley. "Assuming you know how to weed."

Blair slid next to Bump on the picnic bench. "I know how to weed," she said softly.

Bump smiled. "You weed almost as well as you pitch," he said.

"Weeding is fun," Blair said. Then she sighed, and rested her head on Bump's arm.

I was already halfway through my hamburger but I bowed my head and gave thanks for all the wonderful things in my life.

The blessings of our garden.

A stomach that wasn't ripped up.

One friend who loved to eat vegetables and another friend who loved to weed them.

A father you could be yourself with.

● ● ● ● ●

We got the shock of the series when we arrived at the field that night.

"What's Hambone doing here?" I yelped.

"Not just Hambone, it's the whole craphead team," Ivy said. The Terminators of Central Massachusetts were unloading from vans and taking the field.

"Don't you guys ever check the bracket?" Julie said. "We're playing them!"

"But what are they doing here?" I asked. "We beat them in the Qualifier! They're supposed to be back in New England, being second-best."

"A team from New Jersey had to drop out," Mrs. Loomer explained. "The Commissioner gave them a berth because of their close finish in our Qualifier."

"Are you kidding me?" Ivy said. "They stink out loud!"

"If they—as you put it—stunk out loud, they wouldn't have advanced this far," Mrs. Loomer said.

"Well, we're gonna knock them out," I swore. "*Terminate* them!"

Mrs. Loomer smiled, shaking her head. "Forget all the tough talk and just play a good game."

● ● ● ● ●

We lost the coin toss so we were up first. Hambone was on the mound for the Terminators, her pink hair glowing orange under the lights.

Ivy was called out on a strike three at her nose—five

inches out of the zone. She said a string of words that would have gotten me grounded for a month.

"I don't like to hear that talk on my ball field," the umpire growled. "Watch your mouth, batter."

"What? Like you watch the strike zone, Blue?" Ivy snarled. "Maybe you're not deaf, but you're sure blind. And man, are you dumb!"

Ivy got tossed.

She wasn't going to leave quietly. She told the umpire exactly what she thought of him, then she started on Mr. Reed when he tried to get her to leave the field. Finally Bump limped onto the field and waved Ivy off.

Once a cop, always a cop, I thought.

With Jess out of action, Leigha batted in the number two spot. She put down a nice bunt and made it safely to first by a whisker.

"OUT!" the base ump bellowed.

"OUT?" Mr. Reed bellowed. "She was safe, Blue!" He started to cross the lines but Mrs. Loomer pulled him back.

What a way to start the game, I thought. *Two cheap outs, Ivy tossed, Mr. Reed ready to blow.*

I was up next. The first pitch almost took my knee off. I jumped out of the way but the ball hit my bat. "Strike one!" the umpire called.

"What the heck!" Ms. O'Riley shouted from the crowd.

It was an evil pitch but a righteous call. I was just glad the ball went foul.

I crowded closer to the plate. They don't call me MadCat for nothing.

The next one came inside, too. I had to suck in my gut to keep from getting clipped. "Ball one," the ump called.

I crowded even closer, staring at Hambone like she was the ugliest garden slug I ever had the pleasure of stepping on.

Hambone stared back. I smiled. *Go ahead, take a piece of me, you dung beetle.*

She threw—a high strike on the outside corner.

Gotcha. I blasted the ball to left field and took second base standing up.

"Murder-ize it!" I yelled to Bridget. A single could score our first run.

Bridget stood in at the plate, grinning. She'd gotten four hits already today off pitchers from California and Georgia—no pitcher from snowy Massachusetts was going to shut her down.

Hambone knocked her down instead, with a pitch to the leg.

Bridget limped to first base while the plate umpire called the coaches to the pitcher's circle.

"I hope that wasn't on purpose, pitcher," the umpire said.

"It wasn't, I swear!" Hambone said. She sounded like she was crying. "I'm just not warmed up yet."

"You're a real hero," Mr. Reed yelled at Beefsteak. "Can't beat us fairly so you beat up on us!"

"That's bull! These people schedule us for back-to-back games and don't leave us time to get our pitcher ready," Coach Beefsteak barked back. "We play a clean game."

"Now there's a truckload of manure," Mr. Reed said. "You go gunning for my best players, you're going to be sorry."

"Enough!" the umpire yelled. "Let's play ball!"

Two outs, two on, and Blair Reed came up to bat.

Hambone gave her three outside pitches, all off the plate.

On the fourth pitch, Mr. Reed gave her the *take* sign. Blair must have missed it—she swung, hitting a dribbler to Hambone's glove side.

Hambone dug for the ball while Blair dug for the base. Hambone stretched and threw—off the mark! Her throw clipped Blair on the shoulder.

The umpire ruled the ball dead, and awarded us an extra base. That put me at home, scoring the first run.

I expected Mr. Reid to storm Coach Beefsteak or the umpire. Instead, he yelled at Blair for missing his sign.

Hambone apologized profusely. "I was nervous," she called to Blair at first base. Blair ignored her.

She could have been telling the truth, I knew. Some pitchers were like that—the better the batter, the worse they pitched. And some pitchers get such an adrenaline rush when they field a ball, that they can't make the simple throw to first base.

As I expected, Hambone easily struck out Tori.

We took the field in the bottom of the first inning, ahead by one run.

With the way our luck was going, we'd need about twenty more before we could relax.

Chapter TWENTY-EIGHT

Even though Blair struck out the first four batters, two of them got walked anyway.

Ivy was right. The umpire had to be blind. It happened sometimes—you get an official past her prime or too vain to wear his glasses under his mask. You just don't expect one of them at Nationals.

Mr. Reed smashed his clipboard across his knee, breaking it.

With two on and two out, Hambone came to bat. Mr. Reed called time and met us in the pitcher's circle.

"It's time for you to take control of this game," Mr. Reed said to his daughter. Without waiting for a response or looking at me, he went back to the dugout.

"I don't understand," I said.

"You don't have to," Blair said, biting her lip. "Just set up high and inside."

High and inside? As I squatted back in position, I realized Mr. Reed wanted to pay Hambone and Coach Beefsteak back for hitting Bridget and Blair.

I set up high and *outside*.

Blair shook her head. So I set up low and outside.

Blair tried to wave me in. I didn't move my glove.

She asked the ump for time. "We have a mix-up in signs, Blue. We won't be long."

"Set up right, MadCat," she pleaded. "I need a target."

"Isn't Hambone a big enough target?" I said. "This stinks, Blair."

"This is the game, MadCat. How it works at this level," Blair said. "They sent us a message—we've got to send one back."

"Not this way," I said.

"Yes, this way," Blair said. "Coach said to."

"Well, I don't have to help you," I said. I went back to my position.

"Stay off the plate," I whispered to Hambone but she crowded in closer. I would have admired her for her guts but her stupidity got in my way.

I set up high and outside. Mr. Reed bellowed, "MadCat!" but I didn't move my glove.

It didn't matter. The ball came in high, tight, and inside.

Hambone took it on the helmet.

It happened in a flash but I saw everything in slow and horrible detail.

The umpire pointing at Blair, then the bench—ejecting her from the game.

Mr. Reed running out, screaming with fury.

Coach Beefsteak charging out like a bull.

The umpire getting between them.

Mr. Reed's raising his arm —

—making a fist—

—hitting—

—the umpire—

—Coach Beefsteak—

—then a cop, as the cop tried to pull him away.

Bump tried to leap the fence to help. For once in my life, I was grateful he couldn't do it.

●　●　●　●　●

When it was over, Mr. Reed and Coach Beefsteak were heading to the police station in separate patrol cars.

Blair, as silent as stone, was taken away by her mother. They drove off in the opposite direction that the police cruisers had.

Mom and Ginny took us into the dugout to try to calm us down. Meanwhile, the umpire was in a heated discussion with Mrs. Loomer and the Terminators' assistant coach.

After fifteen minutes, the umpire sent everyone off the playing field except for players and coaches. "Let's finish this game! Two outs, bottom of the first inning," he bellowed.

Hambone took first, loading the bases for the Terminators.

"Take off the equipment, MadCat," Mrs. Loomer said. She waved Kayleigh off the bench.

"Huh?" I said. "Why?"

She handed me the game ball. "We need a pitcher," she said. "And you're the only one left standing."

● ● ● ● ●

The Terminators must have thought they had died and gone to heaven. Jenna, Tori, and Nikki ran their stupid heads off in the outfield as the Terminators pounded the crap out of my pitching.

Last winter, I took up pitching because I decided it was time for me to step out of the catcher's box and into the sunshine. I would have given anything to step off the rubber and back into my equipment.

Kayleigh, who had never caught before, was wearing my sweat-soaked gear. Even though she was scared, she got me through four innings, telling me stupid jokes and giving me lots of bubble gum.

The Terminators "mercied" us in the fifth inning, 13–2. We got the second run on a home run by Kayleigh. She was the only Sting player who went home happy that night. The rest of us felt like throwing up.

We had started our road to Nationals in April, dreaming of glory.

We ended it in August, in a nightmare of bloody puke, battling coaches, and broken spirits.

I wanted to go home to Norwich, bury it all in the garden, and let it rot forever.

STING WINS FIVE GAMES AT FASTPITCH WORLD SERIES

The Northeast Sting made its mark at the National Fastpitch Softball World Series, winning five games before being defeated in the middle of the championship round.

"We exceeded everyone's expectations," said Ginny Page, Sting President. "The girls proved they can beat the best in the country . . .

Chapter TWENTY-NINE

I was so mad, I could spit.

I hurt so much, I could cry.

And I was so sick of being hot. I never wanted to see Kentucky again.

"Take me home," I begged. "And keep the air conditioner on all the way."

Ivy and I gave up our plane tickets to Julie's parents so we could ride home in Bump's van. I didn't want to see Ginny Page for a long time, and I never wanted to see Mr. Reed ever again.

Both Mom and Ms. O'Riley still had four days before they had to go back to work so we took our time going home.

In West Virginia, Ivy, Mom, and I climbed a mountain

while Ms. O'Riley read her magazines, and Bump had a long nap. For supper we had sweet corn, fresh-picked plums, and flank steak marinated in apple cider.

In Pennsylvania, Ms. O'Riley took us to a Six Flags amusement park while Mom and Bump went fishing. Around ten that night, we ate grilled eggplant, river trout, and raspberries on ice cream.

Ivy nagged Mom into driving through New York City instead of taking, what she called "the chicken route north." Bump called someone he knew in the New York Police Department and got us tickets to a Mets game. For supper, we had ballpark franks, potato chips, and carrots that Ms. O'Riley had smuggled in. Ivy almost caught a foul ball but some hefty guy in a Yankees cap steamrollered her.

After the game, Mom and Ms. O'Riley drove all night. We arrived in New Hampshire just as the sun was coming up. Mom dropped Ivy and her mother off in Nashua, then we took the back roads home to Norwich.

When we got home, I ran out to the garden. The vegetables were in their glory.

Shiny purple eggplants hung off their hefty bushes. The tomato plants were so loaded, they looked more red than green. The pumpkin vines sprouted fruit that was dark green but the size of basketballs. The summer squash were full and sun-yellow, the zucchinis long and forest-green. Our pepper bushes looked like Christmas trees that had been hung with fat green, red, orange, and yellow ornaments.

Bump made his way to our fruit trees. "Cat! Come here!"

I ran to him, my arms loaded with tomatoes and squash. My father had made the walk to the far backyard using his cane. The wheelchair was still in the van, under loads of luggage and coolers.

"Look!" Bump pulled down a branch on our Cortland tree. The apples were turning red.

"Summer's almost over," I said.

"Do you mind?" Bump asked.

"Not really," I said.

"It feels good to be home," Bump said. He picked the reddest apple, rubbed it clean, then munched it.

"You bet," I said. I took a huge bite from a tomato. Sweet, tangy juice flooded my mouth, dribbling down my chin.

New Hampshire had everything I could ever want. Sun and snow. Mountains and lakes. Maple syrup and apples. Raspberries and pumpkins.

Why, in a million years, did I ever want to *go National*, when all I needed was right here?

● ● ● ● ●

Jess would be traveling to Boston twice a week to work with a college pitching coach this winter. There was even talk of a student exchange next summer, with Jess going to California to play competitive ball.

"Why, in a million years—" I started to ask. Then I just shut my mouth.

Mr. Reed didn't have to pay a fine or do jail time. He worked out a deal with the judge and National Commissioner. He was suspended from the NFS forever, and ordered to enroll in an anger-management program.

"He's really ticked off about the anger-management thing," Mugger said. She was the only kid that Blair would talk to. "He still says it was all the other guy's fault."

I wondered if Blair's pitching career was over.

"She hasn't decided," Mugger said. "But she won't get to make that decision anyway. Mr. Reed is already looking for a team that plays in one of the other softball associations."

Mugger's team won their league championship. They played in the Friendship Tournament in Concord, coming in second place. Her father had made a case for her trophy and displayed it on their front porch. Her old Sting trophies stayed in her bedroom.

Mellissa had left for college by the time we returned from Nationals. She had to get there early for the fall softball season. Mom drove Mugger and me out to see her the weekend after we got back from Kentucky. Her new teammates went nuts over the first ripe apples from our orchard, as well as the zucchini bread and carrot cake that Bump had made.

When I told Mellissa everything that had happened at Nationals, she just shook her head. "People get nuts," she said. "Don't let them spoil the game for you."

Spoil? Nationals had *destroyed* the game for me. My catcher's stuff had to be growing fungus—I couldn't even make myself unzip my bag to unpack it. Mom was going to hang everything out but Bump said, "No. Let Cat deal with it."

The day after we went to see Mellissa, Mugger showed up with her glove.

"What's that for?" I asked.

"Practice," she said. "Mellissa said we can't stop pitching just because the season is over."

I laughed like a hyena, trying not to cry. "Mugger, I'm never gonna pitch again."

She stood there, smiling so wide that her freckles stretched into her hair. But she didn't leave.

"You want to pitch so much, go do it with Blair," I grumbled.

"You started this," Mugger said. "Remember in April? When you came to my house? So I figure you're supposed to finish it."

"Oh, all right," I said. "You pitch, and I'll catch." But when we started wrist snaps, I automatically snapped with Mugger. When we did the step-and-snaps, I swore I was going to just catch. But catching was boring, so I stepped-and-snapped, too.

By the time we got to full motion, Bump had come out to watch. He started the CD player and kept the beat while the music *bam-bam*-ed and our pitches *slap-slap*-ed.

I couldn't help but love this—the ball in my glove, the

169

ball in my hand, the ball whizzing to Mugger. Then back again, watching Mugger step and windmill, the ball blazing at me, the sharp *SMACK!* as it hit my mitt.

I loved the game, even if I would never, ever, in a million years, play in another competitive tournament.

Mugger and I were just finishing up when Ms. O'Riley dropped Ivy off.

"All right!" Ivy yelled. "I'm glad you're still pitching, MadCat!"

"Why?" I growled. "You looking for a good laugh?"

"Ha-ha," she said. "That, too. But, in case you didn't remember, the season isn't over yet."

"Let me guess," I said. "The Terminators have invited us to the Friendship Tournament."

"Ditto ha-ha's," Ivy said. "Check your schedule. We still have one more tournament before school starts. Don't you remember? The Summer-Slam in Tewksbury."

The Summer-Slam was the biggest and best tournament of the summer. The Sting always went, as did most of the tournament teams in New Hampshire and Massachusetts. I loved going to Tewksbury to finish the summer. At least, I used to love it.

"We're not going to that," I said.

"Why not?" Ivy asked.

"For one thing, we don't have a coach," I said.

"We'll find one," Ivy said.

"We don't have a team," I said. "No one's gonna want to go, not after Nationals."

"We'll ask them," Ivy said.

"And we don't have pitchers," I said. "Blair refuses to pitch, and Jess isn't allowed to pitch, not for another month."

"Who needs Her Majesty and the Crown Princess?" Ivy said.

"We do," I said.

"No, we don't," Ivy said. "We've got Bandit, here."

"That's Mugger," I said.

"Whatever," Ivy said. "And we've got you."

"Drop dead," I said.

Ivy just laughed.

Chapter THIRTY

Ivy called a team meeting at my house. Blair was invited but she refused to come. All the rest of the Sting was there to consider the Summer-Slam.

No parents were allowed.

"Come on," Ivy said. "We've got to play again. We can't end the season stinking up the state!"

"We didn't stink up New Hampshire," Jenna said. "We stunk up Kentucky."

"And we didn't even stink up Kentucky," Nikki added. "We finished nineteenth out of more than a hundred teams. That's pretty good."

"Besides, the Summer-Slam is already paid for," Ivy argued. "We might as well go and have fun."

"I vote we go!" Kayleigh shouted. Since her home run

against the Terminators, she was convinced she could do it again, if only given the chance.

"I second it," Bridget cried out.

"All in favor?" Ivy asked.

"Wait!" I yelled. "Jess can't vote because she can't play."

"I can play," Jess said. "I just can't pitch. Or throw overhand."

"All in favor?" Ivy asked again.

There were ten votes *for*: Ivy, Jess, Nikki, Jenna, Erin, Tori, Julie, Kayleigh, Bridget, and Leigha.

I outvoted them with my one vote. "Go ahead," I said. "But I'm not going."

"We need you to pitch!" Erin said.

"You pitch," I said.

"I don't know how!" Erin cried.

"And neither do I," I said.

• • • • •

"MadCat, you're a good pitcher," Mellissa said. Ivy had called her and begged her to persuade me to go to Tewksbury. "You should try it. It will be good experience."

"I've already had plenty of experience at stinking," I said.

"You're full of horse poop," Mellissa said. "You don't stink."

"You're right, I don't stink," I said. "I STINK ROYALLY!"

"Don't exaggerate. You're getting quite decent."

"Passable, maybe," I argued. "But I'm not a Blair Reed. Or a Jess Page."

"And aren't you glad about that?" Mellissa asked.

I didn't say anything.

"What about Mugger?" Mellissa finally asked.

"What about her?" I said.

"She's worked hard all summer. Doesn't she deserve a chance to prove what she can do with a tournament team?"

"She doesn't want to get humiliated any more than I do!" I shouted.

"Youch! My ear!" Mellissa moaned.

"Sorry."

"Who says Mugger would be humiliated?" Mellissa asked.

"I do," I said, too quickly.

"So you think she stinks?"

"I didn't mean that," I said. "I just mean—tournament ball is a lot tougher than rec ball. You said so yourself."

"And a tournament team is a lot better than a rec team," Mellissa said.

"Yeah, exactly," I said. "Mugger and I would just get creamed."

"Not exactly," Mellissa said. "Mugger and you would have one of the best fielding teams in the Northeast behind you."

"Yeah, but—"

"MadCat, did it ever occur to you that fastpitch softball is played by nine players? Not just the pitcher and the catcher?"

"I know that," I said.

But, when it came down to it, I really didn't *believe* that. Jess and I had been pitching and catching since we were little kids. Our softball world had always started at her pitcher's rubber and ended at my mitt.

Everyone else was just like—well, sugar on strawberries. Nice, but not really necessary.

"MadCat?"

"I'm still here," I said.

"What do you think?" Mellissa said. "Why not give it a try? Have some fun, like you used to?"

"I'll ask Mugger," I promised.

I was safe, I thought. Mugger would say no, for sure.

● ● ● ● ●

Mugger said yes.

"Are you nuts?" I yelled.

"Are you selfish?" Blair asked.

"Are you Mugger's mouth?" I snapped.

Blair's eyes filled with tears.

This was the first time I had seen Blair since Kentucky. "I'm sorry," I said. "But why did you say I was selfish?"

"Because of us, and people like my father and Ginny, Mugger got bounced off the Sting," Blair said. "If she's willing to join again for the last tournament, then why should you stop her?"

"You know what happened to me in Kentucky! I got humiliated!" I cried.

"No, *you* got beat," Blair said. "*I* got humiliated."

I was still thinking it over when Jess came by. She had a pair of small socks, sealed in a plastic bag. The socks looked grimy. "Look," she said.

"Whose are these?"

"Yours, MadCat."

"Oh yeah, like my big toe is going to fit into those."

"Your whole foot used to."

"Your brain is still dizzy from blood loss, Jess. I have no clue what you're talking about."

"These are your socks from our first year with the Sting. Remember?"

Jess opened the bag, and pushed the socks into my hands. They were brown with dirt and stiff with what had to be old sweat. There was a hole in one toe. It started to come back to me, being the youngest player on the team and Jess a brand-new pitcher—the Sting would put us in to play only when they were way behind or when the game didn't matter. Jess didn't throw many strikes and I didn't catch many that hit the dirt. But we played hard.

I was so proud to be on the Sting, I didn't change my socks all season. Mom made me wear clean socks to the ballpark but Jess would hide my dirty ones in her bag so I could put them on when we took the field.

It seemed so long ago. "Let me guess. You found them under your bed and want them out of your house so your room will stop stinking."

"Nah," Jess said. "They've been in my bat bag this whole time. I didn't tell you because I thought you'd want them back. They even came to Kentucky with us."

"Oh," I said. "So what's the deal? Why are you bringing them out now?"

"I wanted you to know that just because a lot of things changed, not everything did."

"Oh." I couldn't say anything smarter than that because my throat was suddenly scratchy.

"Okay if I keep them?" Jess's eyes were bright and blinky.

"If you don't mind the smell."

"They smell like softball. Good."

"Can't argue with that," I said.

"So stop trying," Jess said.

And I did.

● ● ● ● ●

We asked Bump to be our coach. "I can't," he said. "That complex is huge—I'd have to—" He rubbed his face. "I just can't."

"Neither can I," I said. "But I'm going to try."

Bump rubbed his face again. When he took his hands away, he was smiling. "Okay," he said. "If you can, then so can I."

Sam Murphy fixed up an old golf cart so my father wouldn't have to maneuver the wheelchair through the ruts and paths between the fields. But it turned out that Bump didn't need the cart. His cane and his team got him where he needed to go.

We kept the golf cart though—it was great for lugging equipment.

"Hey! Know what? We can use the cart to carry our trophies when we win the championship round," Kayleigh gushed.

Trophies? I would be happy to make it out of the Summer-Slam with my head, thank you.

Chapter THIRTY-ONE

It was the Thursday morning before the Summer-Slam. Bump and I were harvesting the garden, loading boxes with ripe vegetables. Whatever we couldn't eat, can, or freeze would go to the Nashua Food Pantry.

We weren't surprised to see Blair appear on our patio. But we were surprised to see Mrs. Reed with her. Bump grabbed his cane and limped out to meet her.

Blair joined me in picking green beans.

"What are you doing here? Did you change your mind about playing?" I asked.

"No," Blair said. "I'm done for this summer."

"So what's up?"

"I have something I have to do," Blair said. She turned her back to me, picking in silence.

A few minutes later, Bump called me to the patio. "Get cleaned off," he told me. "We're going for a ride."

Forty miles later, we arrived in Leominster, Massachusetts. Mrs. Reed had driven us, making polite conversation about the Boston Red Sox the whole way.

Blair and I were in the backseat. Neither of us felt like talking.

"This is it," Bump said. We stopped in front of a white Cape-style house with sky-blue shutters. There was a basketball hoop nailed to the garage and a skate ramp in the side yard.

Bump opened his car door.

"No," Blair said. "I'll go myself."

Mrs. Reed started to protest but Bump waved her quiet.

As tall and strong as Blair was, as she went up the front walk, she looked like a lost kid. "Blair! Wait!" I yelled. I raced to catch up with her.

"You don't have to do this with me," Blair said.

"We're teammates, aren't we?" I asked.

Blair shrugged, then pressed the doorbell.

A big woman with thick glasses answered the door. "Pamela!" she hollered down the hall. "That girl is here."

A few seconds later, Hambone peeked at us from over her mother's shoulder. Her pink hair was now shamrock green. "Hi," she said. She wore glasses almost as thick as her mother's.

"Hi," I said. Blair was frozen silent.

"Outside," her mother said. "I just washed the floor."

She steered Hambone onto the steps with us, then closed the door.

No one said anything for about half a minute. Finally I said, "You look different without your uniform."

"You do too," Hambone said. She towered over me and probably weighed as much as Leigha and Kayleigh put together. But her voice was tiny and high, like a little girl's.

"So, how did you end up in Nationals?" I asked.

"Got smeared in the next game we played," she said. "Came home probably the next day after you guys."

Something knocked my knuckles. I glanced down. Blair was reaching for my hand. Even though she was taller than me, when I took her hand, I felt like the older sister.

Or like the parent who wasn't there—but should have been, I realized.

"You guys going to Summer-Slam?" I asked.

"No," she said. "Our coach got suspended for the rest of the season. None of the other parents wanted to take the team. What about you guys?"

"A bunch of us are," I said. "But not everyone can make it."

Blair's hand shook in mine. I squeezed to keep her steady.

"Well, good luck," Hambone said.

"Yeah," I said.

Blair let go of my hand. I was suddenly afraid she was going to jump off the steps, run down the street, and never be seen again.

But instead, she stepped between Hambone and me. "Pamela?" she said.

"Pam," Hambone said. "Only my mother calls me Pamela, because I'm named after her mother."

"I'm sorry," Blair said.

"That I'm named Pamela?"

"No," Blair said.

"Then, for what?" Hambone asked.

"For hitting you in Kentucky," Blair said.

"You didn't hit me in Kentucky," Hambone said. "You hit me in the head."

I laughed, a real stupid laugh. Hambone laughed with me. Then she put her hand up to Blair for a high five.

I poked Blair. She put her hand up, and accepted Hambone's high five.

"Anyway, I'm sorry," Blair said.

"It really didn't hurt," Hambone said. "The helmet—guess those ugly things really work."

"I shouldn't have done it," Blair said. "I won't do it ever again."

"I wish I could say that," Hambone said. "My control stinks half the time. Maybe you could tell me sometime how you throw all those strikes."

"Sure," Blair said. "Do you have e-mail?"

"Is the sky blue?" Hambone asked.

"Is Kentucky hot?" I said.

We all laughed stupid laughs again.

Hambone gave Blair and me her e-mail address. We

gave her a big box of vegetables, plus a bag of apples and pears. You would have thought it was Christmas.

"I love spinach!" Hambone said. "And squash. Eggplant! Oh cool, there's even lima beans in here. Ever try them with some curried butter? They are so awesome!"

If she didn't have bright green hair, I probably would have hugged her.

We said good-bye and promised to keep in touch. I was already mentally composing an e-mail to nicely suggest she wear her glasses when she pitched. She could probably hit the strike zone more often if she could actually see it.

As Mrs. Reed drove away, I poked Blair. "The *W* goes in the book under your name," I whispered.

"For what?"

"For *winner*," I said.

"What did I win?" Blair asked.

"A friend," I said.

Blair smiled the kind of smile that would mush Mugger's freckles together.

• • • • •

We went to the Summer-Slam with Mugger taking Blair's place on the Sting roster.

School was starting on Tuesday, but that weekend, summer was still ours. The weather was late-August awesome, with blue skies, sunny days, and cool nights. The umpires were all in a good mood, the other teams were

friendly, and even the snack bar hamburgers were edible—
if you had a nice spinach salad to go with them.

We made the parents drop us off in the morning, then
pick us up after the last game at night. They were allowed to
watch any game but ours. The only adults allowed at our
field were Bump and Sam Murphy.

We figured we owed it to Mugger.

Mr. Page took Ginny and the kids to Montreal for the
weekend. Jess stayed with us and even ate some fried eggplant—after she smothered it with ketchup and cheese.

Mugger said Mr. Reed had gone to California on a business trip. She told us that, while he was gone, Mrs. Reed had
ripped up the tuition check for Nicholls. Then she regis-
tered Blair at Nissitissit Middle School.

Bump let us make our own lineup for each game.
Everyone played and everyone took turns sitting on the
bench. We taught our friends from Dracut, Chelmsford,
and Hudson all the new cheers we had learned in Kentucky.

I pitched half the games, Mugger pitched the other half.
Ivy caught for Mugger and Kayleigh caught for me.
Kayleigh didn't bobble a ball once. "Mr. Reed almost gave
me an ulcer," she told me when I complimented her on her
improved glove work. "Your father doesn't expect me to
mess up. So I don't."

Jess played right field or second base. When she needed
to make a throw, she shoveled the ball underhand to Bridget
at first base, and Bridget threw it for her.

Leigha made a ton of impossible stops. Erin made one

or two herself. The fielders were very, very busy, proving to all of Massachusetts and New Hampshire—and Mugger and me—that they were, indeed, among the best around.

We lost half our games. But we won half, too. It's not important which half, because they were all fun—every inning of every game—but just for the record, we were third runners-up.

We didn't get a trophy for that. But we did get T-shirts that said:

EATING DIRT IS BETTER THAN LOSING.

Nice shirts, but they got it wrong. They should have read:

EATING DIRT IS WHAT YOU DO FOR YOUR TEAM, WIN OR LOSE.

Coming in third in the Summer-Slam was the happiest moment of my life because my team was there, all of whom—including Mugger—were my best friends in the whole state of New Hampshire.

And *that* is how you really play the game.